robot
graveyard.

the wizard's
eye

CARTOGRAPHER'S
• HILL

fallingstar
road

ESERT

SHWORKS

athered funicula

pokenose
peak

Pfefferminz Ridge

CURSEWORKS

mines of
orrow

• realm of the
spider lords

• SCORPIUS
HARBOR

RECHAUN
OUNTY ❧

nooplewhoop's
verlasting
ircus

• shaleleigh

N

W   E

S

The Misadventures of
Benjamin Bartholomew Piff

3 Wishing Well

Written and illustrated by
Jason Lethcoe

Grosset & Dunlap

Cover illustration by Katrina Damkoehler

GROSSET & DUNLAP
Published by the Penguin Group
Penguin Group (USA) Inc., 375 Hudson Street, New York, New York 10014, USA
Penguin Group (Canada), 90 Eglinton Avenue East, Suite 700, Toronto,
Ontario M4P 2Y3, Canada
(a division of Pearson Penguin Canada Inc.)
Penguin Books Ltd., 80 Strand, London WC2R 0RL, England
Penguin Group Ireland, 25 St. Stephen's Green, Dublin 2, Ireland
(a division of Penguin Books Ltd.)
Penguin Group (Australia), 250 Camberwell Road, Camberwell, Victoria 3124, Australia
(a division of Pearson Australia Group Pty. Ltd.)
Penguin Books India Pvt. Ltd., 11 Community Centre, Panchsheel Park,
New Delhi—110 017, India
Penguin Group (NZ), 67 Apollo Drive, Rosedale, North Shore 0745, Auckland, New Zealand
(a division of Pearson New Zealand Ltd.)
Penguin Books (South Africa) (Pty.) Ltd., 24 Sturdee Avenue,
Rosebank, Johannesburg 2196, South Africa

Penguin Books Ltd., Registered Offices:
80 Strand, London WC2R 0RL, England

Library of Congress Control Number is available.

ISBN 978-0-448-44498-7   10 9 8 7 6 5 4 3 2 1

This book is for Mustafa Pez, Viktor VonRiesling, Renson Whistlestick, Newton Fripp, Daedalus Erdanase, Theophilus Netherlands, Maxiumus, and, of course, my good friend Phineas Crumpt.

Keep the Key, Bury the Head, Drink the Light.

Acknowledgments

This book wouldn't be possible without the continuous love and support of my wife, Nancy, and my kids, Emily, Alex, and Olivia. Also, I would like to thank my brother JP for his thought-provoking podcast, "What Are You Doing?" Thanks for providing me with hours of entertainment while I spend my time at Wishworks.

TABLE OF CONTENTS

CHAPTER ONE
Mahdi's Wish

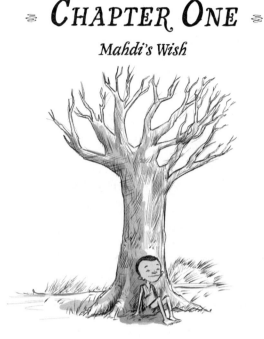

Mahdi cupped a handful of dirt in his small, brown hand and let the hot earth trickle between his fingers. It had been three months since the Kenyan village of Kumahumato had seen any rain.

"Mahdi!" He heard his father's tired voice call to him. Mahdi rose from under the old acacia tree and trotted over to the doorway of his house.

"Yes, Abu?" he said, using the Kiswahili word for "Daddy."

"I want you to take this down to the market and buy whatever food and water you can with it." His father handed him a twenty-shilling coin. Mahdi was only ten, but he was old enough to know that twenty shillings would not buy very much.

Mahdi nodded. He pocketed the coin and set off down the road, his bare feet kicking up tiny dust clouds as he walked. The village looked deserted, but Mahdi knew that the stillness was due to the fact that most people were crowded inside their tiny huts, trying to stay cool.

After a few minutes of walking, Mahdi spotted a large, dry well on the side of the road. At one time, people had come to this big well to water their camels and livestock. But not anymore. The name Kumahumato meant "that which supports cattle," but it had been a long time since the village had lived up to its name.

Something attracted Mahdi to the well. He walked over and peered inside. Maybe he should try lowering the bucket, in case there was water at the bottom.

He could hear his father's voice in his mind, telling him not to get his hopes up. Living in a place that had droughts and terrible floods had taught most of the poor villagers that hope was a luxury they couldn't afford. Miracles didn't happen in Kumahumato. Life was hard, and anyone who spent time dreaming that it could be any different was foolish. Nothing would ever change.

But Mahdi disagreed with them.

Wishes can come true, he assured himself. Sometimes grown-ups forgot that.

His hand moved to the coin that rested in his pocket.

Mahdi knew that he had to use the twenty shillings to buy water. His mind drifted to thoughts of the others in his family—his cousin Abdi, whose mother had died of fever last week, and his baby sister Nathifa, whose thirsty whimpers kept him awake most nights.

But what if . . .

He took the coin from his pocket and watched the sunlight reflect off its surface. What he was about to do would get him into deep trouble, but he couldn't help it. Something had pulled him toward the well.

I wish this well was full of water and that our village wouldn't be thirsty anymore, Mahdi thought with his eyes shut.

He tossed the coin into the well, watching it glitter as it tumbled down into the darkness. He listened for any sound of a splash as it hit the bottom.

Mahdi didn't hear anything.

Please let my wish come true, Mahdi thought desperately as he walked back down the dusty road to the village. He had never wanted anything so badly.

❂ ❂ ❂

A pair of glowing red eyes pierced the gloom at the bottom of the well. Moments later, a twisted hand with broken, yellow fingernails emerged from a secret tunnel and snatched the golden coin from where it had fallen on the muddy earth.

The dry well was not empty after all.

⸙ CHAPTER TWO ⸙

Flight of Fancy

Benjamin Bartholomew Piff soared above the Wishworks Factory in his magical, winged chair. Even though he was afraid of heights, he couldn't help but grin at the rush he felt as the chair flapped above the clouds.

But wait . . . hadn't all of the Feathered Funicula chairs been destroyed by his evil cousin Penelope Pauline Piff in the last Wishworks War? If so, how could he be flying in one of those chairs now?

Ben needed time to think. He nudged the control stick forward, leveling the chair into a gentle glide.

Ben remembered that a powerful Jinn named Hoccus had provided Wishworks with the original plans to rebuild the Feathered Funicula, the massive tower that held the winged chairs. But the rebuilding progress was slow. The chairs had been around for hundreds of years. And nobody in living memory had ever had to build one from scratch before. The amount of Jinn magic needed to build even one chair was taking all of the resources the partially destroyed Factory could manage.

Suddenly, Ben noticed something moving by the eastern wall of the Factory below him. He moved the control stick forward and banked the Feathered Funicula chair into a gentle dive to take a closer look.

As he moved in, he spotted the last person he ever expected to see. A round-faced girl with long braids and a sour expression was leading a procession of scuttling creatures through a crack in the Wishworks wall. It was his dreaded cousin Penelope Piff and an army of Curseworks' Spider Monkeys!

Ben knew that his evil cousin and her half-spider, half-monkey army were getting ready to attack the Factory. He had to warn Thomas Candlewick, the president of Wishworks!

Ben quickly flew to the President's Tower. But when he reached Candlewick's office, he was nowhere to be found. After a few seconds of searching, Ben spotted a note pinned to Candlewick's chair. With a horrible, sinking feeling, he read the words written in hot pink ink:

YOU'LL NEVER SEE HIM ALIVE AGAIN!

Ben realized the awful truth.

Thomas Candlewick had been kidnapped by Penelope!

This can't be happening again!

It was only a few weeks earlier that Candlewick had suddenly disappeared from the Factory because of his cousin Penelope's twelfth birthday wish. The evil girl had become president of the Factory and had transformed it into a factory that gave out curses instead of wishes!

Ben was confused. He remembered rescuing Candlewick and defeating Penelope. How could this be happening all over again?

Ben began to panic. He didn't know what to do. But he did know one thing: He was still the manager of Kids' Birthday Wishes: Ages 3 to 12. And it was up to him to save the president and the Factory!

≈ CHAPTER THREE ≈

The Meeting

"**W**hat does it take to wake you up, a troop of Spider Monkeys?" Ben's eyes flicked open as he felt two tiny hands roughly shaking him awake.

"Huh?" Ben mumbled.

"I tried to call you for five minutes straight!" Nora said. "There are probably a dozen messages on your voice mail."

Ben shook his head. "But what about Candlewick?" he asked, still confused.

Nora sighed. "Exactly my point. If we don't hurry, we're gonna be late for our meeting."

"What meeting?" Ben asked.

"Hello? The meeting with Candlewick?" Nora said, crossing her arms. "Boy, that's the last time we stay out late at the Wing and a Prayer Café. You must have had one too many Flooper Fizzes[1] last night."

The meeting! Wow, he must have been dreaming before. Ben leaped out of bed. How could he have forgotten?

"Got it!" Ben said. "Let me get dressed. I'll meet you at Candlewick's office in five minutes."

He washed and dressed at lightning speed. Minutes later, he was racing down the broken cobblestone streets that led to Thomas Candlewick's office, holding his oversize top hat firmly with one hand.

Ben took the stairs that led up to the Presidential Office two at a time. He hoped that Candlewick, who insisted on punctuality, wouldn't be too upset that he was running a few minutes late.

"Did I make it?" Ben asked breathlessly as he closed the big doors behind him. The Wishworks president glanced at his ornate pocket watch and gave Ben a tired grin.

"Almost." He stood up and stretched. Ben could tell that

---

[1] Flooper Fizz, an unusual beverage that, among its other qualities, has been known to make the regular drinker grow a sixth toe, is the favorite soft drink at Wishworks.

the strain of trying to get Wishworks back up and running was taking its toll on the forty-year-old president. Ben could have been imagining it, but it looked like his salt-and-pepper hair seemed to have gotten much grayer in the last few months.

Moments later, a tiny knock on the huge wooden doors of Candlewick's office interrupted Ben's thoughts. Nora, dressed in a suit of forest green and sporting her broad-brimmed, pointed hat, ran into the office. Jumping up on the leather couch, she said, "Sorry I'm late! Fizzle stopped me on the way over. She tried to get me to sample some crazy new gum she's invented."

Fizzle, Ben and Nora's fairy friend, had been spending a lot of time with her sick grandfather, who owned Fizzypop's Gum Shop. The shop was famous for its magical gum, and Fizzle had been busy trying to create some incredible new formulas of her own.

"No problem," Candlewick said. Then, after snapping his magical pocket watch shut, he moved from behind his desk and sat down on an oversize chair.

"Okay," Candlewick said, looking intently at Ben and Nora. "When was the last time I updated you on the situation with the Jinns?"

Ben and Nora exchanged glances.

"Um, the last thing I heard was a couple weeks ago, when you said that we had sent a messenger to Snazz' Madoodle[2] outlining a new contract proposal," Ben said, shrugging his shoulders.

Ben knew that the Wishworks president had been desperately trying to repair the damaged relationship with the Jinns. When Penelope Piff had taken over Wishworks, one of the first things she did was imprison a Jinn in a magic lamp. Unfortunately, her actions destroyed the years of hard work that Thomas Candlewick had put into regaining the Jinns' trust. Jinns had a long history of not trusting humans. And after the experience with Penelope, the Jinns' mistrust of humans had been renewed. They had abandoned the Factory, leaving an already damaged Wishworks with barely enough magic to fulfill the wishes that flooded in every day.

Candlewick opened a drawer on a nearby end table and removed a large envelope. He tossed it to Ben, who opened it and saw the burned remains of Candlewick's proposal. Ben also noticed that several pieces of the charred paper had

---

[2] After the Jinns' capital city, now known as Snazz' Madoodle, was built in 494 A.D., a contest was held to decide what to name it. The legends say that none of the names that the citizens came up with did the beautiful city justice. Then, just as the people were about to give up and resign themselves to living in a nameless city, a child sneezed out the word "SNAZZ' MADOODLE!" The name has stuck ever since.

Jinnish symbols scrawled over them in red ink.

"So I guess they didn't like it," Ben said, handing the envelope back to Candlewick.

Candlewick shook his head grimly and replaced the envelope in the drawer. "No, they did not. And if we can't figure out a way to make peace with the Jinns, they'll declare war."

"But I don't get it," Nora said. "This is all Ben's cousin's fault. *She* was the one who enslaved a Jinn in a lamp. Why are they blaming *us*?"

"You have to understand the Jinns' way of thinking," Candlewick replied. "It might seem like ancient history to us, but many of them haven't forgotten being enslaved. A huge part of the Jinn population is old enough to remember back thousands of years, when they were forced to obey any human who controlled their lamp. Even though we have treated the Jinns as equals here at Wishworks, they think that all humans are capable of forcing them back into the lamps."

"I still don't get how Penelope even found one of the lamps. I thought that they had all been destroyed," Ben said.

Candlewick nodded. "So did I. But somehow she got her hands on one. I don't know how she did it."

"Couldn't she just have wished for one?" Ben asked.

Candlewick shook his head. "Wouldn't have worked. There's no way a wish like that could have been processed through the Factory. The magical contract with the Jinn labor union would have prevented it." Candlewick sighed and continued. "It was during the term of President Cheeseweasle that the whole issue about lamps got out of control. There was a large group of Jinns that claimed that the magic lamps had never truly been destroyed and that Wishworks was hiding them in a secret chamber underneath the Factory. Cheeseweasle defended Wishworks' position that the lamps had been destroyed long ago. He refused to let the Jinns dig underneath the Factory. He claimed that it would upset the gnomes who control the Wishing Well Pipeline."

"Hold on. Did you say 'Wishing Well Pipeline'?" Ben looked confused. "What's that?"

"It's an intricate network of pipes that connects all of the Wishing Wells around the world," Nora explained. "My dad used to talk about it all the time. The gnomes gather the coins that are thrown into every Wishing Well and send the wishes to Wishworks. Then, after the wishes are granted, the gnomes take the coins and melt them down to make their incredible inventions. They make new weapons to help defend the Factory, and also lots of the complicated toys and mechanical gadgets that people wish for."³

Candlewick nodded. "Your dad is right. But the Jinns thought that Cheeseweasle was working with the gnomes to hide the magic lamps. They declared war on Wishworks and recruited the help of Abul Cadabra and his Lamp of One Thousand Nightmares."

"And that's when Penelope Thicklepick and Finneas Cheeseweasle came up with the four weapons that saved the Factory, right?" Ben asked.

"In *Wishworks Presidents, Past and Present,* it says that they came up with the ideas for the Impeacher, the Cornucopia, the Thumper, and the Whirling Whizzy." Candlewick paused and gave Ben and Nora a conspiratorial grin. "But what the book doesn't mention is who actually designed and built the weapons."

---

³ One of the gnomes' more recent gadgets is the "Cell" phone, named for its inventor, a gnome with very large ears, named Cellington Mobilemaker. At first, the invention seemed to be a terrific accomplishment, and the gnomes were pleased by the humans' enthusiastic response after the phone was introduced. However, there is a fatal flaw in the technology. Cellington used a metal called Jabberonium when he created the phone, a metal that has since proved to have strange addictive powers to many humans. This metal is especially dangerous for teenage girls, and there are well-documented cases where the Jabberonium addiction was so strong that the phone became permanently fused to the young person's ear. Research is underway in the Gnomish labs to remedy the problem.

"Was it the gnomes?" Nora asked.

"Exactly." Candlewick nodded. "Only the gnomes would have been able to design weapons of such genius and power."

Candlewick stood up and began to pace around the office. "Our spies have recently returned from a mission to the Jinn Territories. The news they brought back wasn't good. There is a rumor floating around that the Jinns are looking for a way to find Abul Cadabra's lamp and bring him back. The Jinns think that if Penelope used one of the lamps, then there must be other lamps hidden away somewhere. And with Abul Cadabra on their side, they'll destroy Wishworks."

"What are we going to do, Thom?" Ben asked anxiously.

"I'm going on a diplomatic mission to the Jinn Territories," Candlewick told them. "I would like the two of you to go down to the Gnomish city of Tiktokket. We have the Cornucopia and, thanks to your last mission, the Impeacher. Since the last battle, I have been spending every minute searching through the Wishworks Archival Museum[4]

---

[4] The museum holds over ten million exhibits. Its slogan, "Don't just spend a day visiting the museum, spend a lifetime," was interpreted literally by a boy who entered the museum on a school field trip when he was six years old, and wasn't seen again until he was seventy-five. When he was asked how he liked the museum, he replied, "It got a little boring after exhibit seven million, five hundred thousand sixty-two, but overall, it was a pretty good time."

for any possible clue as to the whereabouts of the last two weapons, the Thumper and the Whirling Whizzy." He sighed and glanced up at Ben and Nora. "We've got to find all four weapons, and fast! If we enter into a war with the Jinns, it's only by using all four weapons together that we can hope to save Wishworks."

Candlewick walked over to his big mahogany desk. He opened a drawer and took out an unusual-looking metal helmet that was covered with brass gears.

"Yesterday I checked out an exhibit of gifts that was sent to past presidents," Candlewick said. "I found this helmet next to a display of Penelope Thicklepick's prized beetle collection."

Candlewick handed the helmet to Ben. Ben examined the strange-looking hat. As he turned it over, he saw some writing:

CLOCKWORK HELMET

PATENT NUMBER 782 BY B. BLASTINGCAPP.

SEE . . . THE . . . 4 . . . LEMENTS . . . USE . . . ITH . . .

AUTION . . .

THAUMAPHOR . . . KEPT.

"There's something written here, but it's hard to read. Some of the words look totally worn off. And what does 'Thaumaphor' mean?" Ben asked.

"That's what I asked Ignatius Crumb, the museum's curator," Candlewick said. "He told me that *Thaumaphor* is a Greek word that means 'That which carries miracles.' As far as the rest of the words go, I can only take a guess. I think it might be something like, 'Seek the 4 Elements. Use with caution to find where the Thaumaphor is kept.' "

Candlewick scratched his long chin thoughtfully. "I think that we've been calling the third weapon by the wrong name. I believe that 'Thaumaphor' is the real name for what we've been calling the 'Thumper.' "

"Thauma. Like in *Thaumaturgic Cardioscope*!" said Nora excitedly. "It makes sense!"

Ben remembered learning about the Thaumaturgic Cardioscope on his first day at Wishworks. The magical machine was capable of tuning in to the heart of any individual anywhere in the world and "listening in" on their secret and most desperate wishes. When Candlewick had first shown him the huge device and had said its name, he'd never even heard the word *Thaumaturgic* before. But since being at Wishworks, he'd heard the word more than once. Recalling the other time he'd heard the strange word, he said, ". . . Or like *Thaumaturgic Cartographers*."

Candlewick shot Ben a sharp look. "Where did you hear that name?"

Ben stared back at Candlewick, startled by the intensity of his question.

"I . . . remembered seeing it when I visited Snooplewhoop's Everlasting Circus. Nora and I had to get Sephira Sparkletoe's poem and use it to rescue you from the Halls of Sleep." Ben fidgeted under Candlewick's intense stare. "That was written on a card next to this creepy shrunken head in his office. Why? Who are they?"

Candlewick looked relieved. "Er, nobody important. Nobody you should worry about, anyway."

Ben couldn't figure out why Candlewick was being so secretive.

"Judging by the craftsmanship and the intricate gears, I'm guessing that the helmet is of Gnomish design," Candlewick said, changing the subject back to the helmet.

Candlewick took the helmet from Ben and gazed at the complicated series of brass gears and switches that decorated the top of its shiny metal surface.

"I would like you to take this helmet with you on your trip," Candlewick said. "I'm hoping that Togglenoggin, the Gnome king, might be able to tell us how it works. It might be useful in helping us locate the Thaumaphor."

Ben and Nora exchanged excited glances as Candlewick continued. "I have already talked to Jeannie and Fizzle, and they have volunteered to go with you. The Wishing Well Pipeline can attract some dangerous creatures, so having extra friends along for protection couldn't hurt. In the meantime, I'll be traveling with Gene and Jonathan to Snazz' Madoodle on a diplomatic mission. Hopefully, talking to the head of the Jinn Union in person will change their feelings."

Ben's relationship with Jeannie, Gene's sister, had always been a little bit strained. The Jinn had always seemed aloof, and Ben thought that she didn't like him very much because he was human. Privately, he wished it could have been just Nora and Fizzle going with him.

"So, when do we leave?" Nora asked.

"Before dawn," said Candlewick. "I don't want anybody to see you or to ask any questions. This mission is top secret. No word of what we're doing can leak out to Curseworks or the Jinns."

Candlewick fixed Ben with a level gaze.

"Ben, you'll be leading this one."

Ben nodded and grinned. The thought of going on a secret mission early in the morning filled him with excitement.

"Nora, you're second in command." Candlewick smiled at the small girl encouragingly. "You'll need to find the Factory's main Wishing Well. It is located at the far western side of the Factory, through a tunnel that hardly anyone uses anymore.

I've instructed Jeannie and Fizzle to meet you there."

Candlewick produced a piece of paper and scribbled down the directions. "Once you go down the Well, it will connect you to a spot in the Pipeline that's only a few miles from the Gnomish city. Remember, don't breathe a word about this mission to anybody."

"Okay," agreed Ben and Nora.

"Good." Candlewick said. He nodded, looking satisfied. "I'm counting on both of you."

ᵉ CHAPTER FOUR ᵉ
An Early Departure

*T*he next morning, Ben leaped out of bed two minutes before his alarm was set to go off. He excitedly threw on his coat and big top hat. Even though it was still dark outside, he was wide awake. He couldn't wait to get started on the day's adventure!

Moments later, he and Nora were walking down misty cobblestone streets lined with Victorian-era gas lamps.

"I've never been to the western part of the Factory before," Ben said. "What's it like?"

"I've only been back there a couple of times. It's pretty

cool. There are lots of weird buildings."

Wishworks was easily as big as a small city, and Ben knew that it would take him years to explore it all.

As they walked, Ben noticed that there were all kinds of Wishworks departments that he hadn't seen yet on this side of the Factory. They passed a big green building with HOLIDAY WISHES written on it in silver letters and then an old, rickety building with the words NEW YEAR'S RESOLUTION DEPT.[5]

Ben and Nora continued following Candlewick's map. After a series of turns, Ben noticed a boomerang-shaped sign hanging over a brick building that was covered with copper pipes. *"Battlerang Research and Development,"* Ben read. "I didn't know this place was here."

"Neither did I," Nora said.

"Couldn't we just stop for a minute and peek inside?" Ben asked. He was thinking about his own Battlerang, which he carried in his back pocket. Maybe he could buy a cool accessory for his magical weapon.

"I don't think it's open. Besides," Nora said, glancing at her watch, "the sun will be up soon, and Candlewick wants us to get to the Well without being seen. We'd better hurry."

---

[5] This department is the busiest in the Factory from the first of January to about the middle of February. The rest of the year, the lucky workers take vacations.

Ben reluctantly followed Nora back down the cobblestone streets. He saw several more interesting-looking departments, including a very creepy building labeled DEATH WISHES.[6] He told himself that he would have to come back and investigate this part of the Factory later.

Finally, they emerged into a clearing. The shadowy outline of tall, crazily shaped trees towered above them. But as they walked on, Ben saw that they weren't trees at all. They were giant stalks that stretched up about fifty feet in the air. And at the tops of the stalks were bushy yellow flowers.

Dandelions. Ben couldn't believe his eyes. Behind the huge flowers sat a building with a large star on top of it. A sign on the building read DANDELION WISH AND FALLING STAR DEPT.

Ben remembered seeing the building from the air when he had first toured the Factory by Feathered Funicula chair. But had never been this close to it before.

"Aha!" Ben heard Nora say. She had spotted the entrance to a huge tunnel.

"The map says that the Well is on the other side of this tunnel," Nora said excitedly.

---

[6] The Death Wish department is seldom visited, largely due to the fact that its workers all work the graveyard shift.

Ben looked at the tunnel's towering archway. It was carved with the figures of tiny bearded gnomes.

"Come on!" Nora glanced anxiously at the sky, which was turning a rosy shade of pink. "Let's get through before the Factory workers wake up."

≈ CHAPTER FIVE ≈
The Wishworks Well

As Ben exited the tunnel, he saw Jeannie and Fizzle standing next to the biggest Wishing Well he'd ever seen.

It's gotta be at least thirty feet high! he thought.

Fizzle flitted forward. "Hi, Ben," she said. "Oooo, is that the helmet? Can I see?"

"Sure." Ben held up the Clockwork Helmet so that the tiny fairy could have a look inside. Fizzle hovered over it, studying the inscription. Her short cropped hair had tiny pink flowers braided into it, and she wore a black T-shirt inscribed with the name of the pixie rock group the Dingleberries.[7]

"Cool!" she said, grinning prettily up at him. Ben blushed. From the moment he had first seen the fairy, he had thought she was cute.

"Let's get going," Jeannie said anxiously. Her smoky tail was a deep crimson color, a sign that she was nervous or upset.

"Okay, okay. Don't get that smoky tail of yours in a knot," Nora teased as she and Ben approached the Well.

"How are you, Jeannie? I haven't seen you in a while," Ben said.

Jeannie flashed Ben a friendly smile. "I'm okay. I've been really busy." She patted Ben on the shoulder. "How have you been? I've heard all kinds of great things about you since you had your promotion to manager of Kids' Birthday Wishes: Ages 3 to 12."

"Thanks," he said. "It's been hard to get the birthday

---

[7] The hardest rocking band in the Land of Faerie is the Dingleberries. Their recent number one hits include "On a Wing and a Prayer," "Humans Don't Know We Exist," and the very popular "Fairy, Fairy Quite Contrary." In a recent interview, bandleader and bagpipe player Colin Pinkytoe was quoted as saying, "The Dingleberries are now more popular than the Stones and the Beatles." This caused an uproar in the fairy community, especially among collectors of small pebbles and entomologists, who claimed that Pinkytoe's statement was "outrageous" and "simply not true."

wishes fulfilled, since, you know . . . the Jinn strike and everything," he said awkwardly.

A flash of something Ben couldn't read flickered over Jeannie's face, but it was soon replaced with a sympathetic smile.

"Well, you shouldn't worry about things you can't control. Just do the best you can."

They were interrupted by Nora, who had climbed up the side of the big Well. "Hey, check this out!" she called.

Ben approached the huge, stone wall and looked over the side. The walls of the Well were at least twenty feet across and plunged way, way down.

"How are we going to get down there?" he asked.

"I guess we should use the bucket," Nora suggested.

"It does look big enough to hold all of us," Ben said.

At that moment, the sound of Wishworks employees entering the other end of the tunnel made everybody jump.

"Oh, great. Somebody's coming!" Nora whispered as she cast a worried glance at the tunnel.

"Quick, get in!" Ben said, climbing into the bucket. "We'll hide in here until they're gone." Nora had barely followed Ben inside when suddenly the big bucket gave a lurch!

Ben and Nora shot each other a horrified glance. Then with a loud *CREAAAK*, the rope that had been supporting the bucket twisted and snapped, plunging the bucket into the darkness below.

"AAAAHHHHH!" they both screamed as the stony walls of the Well rushed past. Ben's stomach twisted with fear as they fell, and he was remotely aware of Nora's tiny fingernails digging into his arm.

SPLASH!

The bucket hit bottom. Ben's teeth rattled from the impact, and his top hat flew off his head. Nora was nearly thrown out of the bucket but managed to stay inside only because of her firm grip on Ben's arm.

After a moment, the leprechaun shakily disentangled herself from Ben and peered over the big bucket's edge.

"Are you guys okay?" Jeannie and Fizzle floated down to them from the Well's opening up above. Jeannie held out Ben's hat.

"I think so," Ben said, rubbing his elbow. "Man, you guys are lucky that you can fly."

Jeannie and Fizzle helped Ben and Nora out of the bucket and onto a nearby stone embankment. Although they were both shaken from the fall, they were not hurt.

"Let's check out where we are," Fizzle said. She pulled out a fairy light from her tiny pack. When she turned it on, the dark bottom of the Well was lit up. A shadowy passageway with a low ceiling stretched to the right of the stone embankment.

"Look," Ben said, pointing to the right. "That seems like some sort of passageway."

"There's something written on the wall," Jeannie said, trying to make out the words. "I haven't studied Gnomish," she muttered apologetically, "but since this appears to be the only way in, I guess we'd better take it."

"Right," Ben said as he moved forward. "Everybody stay close." He was just about to enter the shadowy tunnel when he remembered something. "Oops, I almost forgot the helmet."

He dashed back to the huge bucket and looked inside. His eyes quickly scanned the interior, searching for where he had put the Clockwork Helmet only a few moments before.

It wasn't there! Panicked, he climbed inside and felt around the floor.

"No, no, no!" Ben cried.

"What's the matter?" Nora asked.

"The helmet must have fallen out when we crashed," Ben said miserably. "That water is so deep, I don't know if we can get it out."

Whirr, clunk. Whirr, clunk. Whirr, CLUNK! ROOOOOOAAAAAR!

Ben looked up in alarm as a terrifying sound echoed off

of the cavernous walls of the well.

Ben automatically pulled his Battlerang out of his back pocket. "Battlerangs out, everybody!" he called.

Then, with a horrible feeling in the pit of his stomach, Ben saw a long, creepy shadow edge out of the passageway on their right and heard a low growl.

Ben's heart pounded as he stared at the tunnel's entrance. Whatever was making the noise was coming from inside there. His hand tightened on his Battlerang's handle, ready to attack.

Then the *thing* showed its ugly head. Jeannie, Nora, and Fizzle screamed. Ben gasped as the creature roared, revealing a set of the sharpest teeth he'd ever seen in his life!

CHAPTER SIX
Penelope's Plight

There were terrible, dark secrets that lay within the tomes of the Curseworks Library, and Penelope Pauline Piff was determined to find them all.

After being exiled from Wishworks by her cousin Ben, she had eagerly accepted the offer to become president of Curseworks. From the moment she had first entered the evil Factory, she had felt at home. Though she did make a few changes.

The first thing she had done was redecorate the gloomy Factory with pink wallpaper. And the iron furniture had been covered with pink fur. To complete her theme, she had insisted that her new servants discard their creepy black uniforms and dress entirely in pink. There had been protests from some of the Spider Monkeys when she'd announced the change, but they'd given in after Penelope had threatened them with torture.

Once she had finished these important tasks, she'd headed for the Curseworks Library. She was searching for a nasty spell that she could use to exact revenge on her cousin Ben.

As president of Wishworks, she had tasted the power that she had always longed for. And then she had had to endure the humiliation of having it stripped away. The Wishworks Factory should have been *hers*. After all, she *had* followed all of the wishing rules to a T when she had wished to be Queen of Wishworks on her birthday.[8]

Penelope would have maintained her evil dictatorship if her cousin Ben hadn't interfered. Not to mention the fact that she had lost her precious pet dragon, Sweetums, in the process! It was too much to endure. She had always disliked her cousin, but now she hated him more than ever.

---

[8] The rules for making birthday wishes are as follows: The wish must be made with the eyes closed. The candles must be blown out with a single breath; no spitting, coughing, or sputtering will count. And the wish must never, under any circumstances, be spoken aloud.

"Let's see," she whispered, thumbing through a book titled *1001 Curses for the Truly Wicked*, "a curse that removes the victim's nose and places it on his or her elbow." She stared at the engraving that illustrated the effects of the uncomfortable curse and wrinkled her nose in distaste.

"Too nice," she muttered to herself as she placed the heavy book back on the shelf and looked for something much worse. She was about to grab one titled *Cursing for Fun and Profit* when she spotted the corner of an unusual book that was pushed into a crack in the wall.

As she pulled the small black book off the shelf, a cloud of dust rose up.

"Achoo!" Penelope sneezed, wiping her nose on her pink shirtsleeve. *"The Chosen Two and the Return of Abul Cadabra,"* [9] Penelope said as she read the book's title.

---

[9] Dark rumors surrounded the acquisition of this book by the Curseworks Factory. Most of the employees at Curseworks believed that the book first came to the Factory by President Snivel Buzzsaw (1840–1865), who acquired it by trading a dozen curses to a traveling Jinnish merchant. Others believed the cursed book was found in a cave by the Wretched Grenadiers on a journey through the caves in the Pfefferminz Ridge. The truth of the matter is still debated, but popular modern belief is that it was bought on eBay by Adolfus Thornblood. The ex-president is said to have outbid his opponent, gaining the evil volume for a mere five dollars from an old woman in a trailer park in Phoenix, Arizona. The priceless book is valued among all collectors of truly evil literature, ranking just above the books *Evil Is Fun* and *More Evil, Please* in collectibility.

Penelope knew all about Abul Cadabra's reputation. He was the most powerful curse-maker in history.

Penelope opened the book but was immediately disappointed. The book was written entirely in Jinnish!

A knock on the Library door interrupted her thoughts.

"Yeah, what is it?" she called.

"It is time to test your new invention, Your Majesty," Penelope's adviser, Rottenjaw, said as he swept into the room. She noticed that the attorney looked uncomfortable in his newly acquired pink suit. Penelope grinned maliciously. It made her feel good to see the man squirm.

"It's about time!" Penelope snapped as she quickly shoved the small book into her jeans pocket and strode to the door.

Penelope was sure her cousin Ben underestimated how efficiently she had been spending her time at Curseworks during the weeks since her army's defeat.

Among the first tasks she had taken on when she'd become the Factory's newest and youngest president[10] was finding a way to power its terrible, curse-making machinery. Adolfus

---

[10] The youngest president of Curseworks before Penelope was Thurston Nosegrinder (1974–1985), who inherited the Factory from his father, Pinchnose. He was only fourteen and is famous for creating the concept of "year-round schools," a curse that still persists and eliminates summer breaks for suffering school-age children everywhere.

Thornblood, the last president of Curseworks, had kept all of the sources of power for the machines a secret. It had taken Penelope quite some time to figure out a way to make them work, but an idea had come to her. If it was successful, she would finally be able to send the vicious, dragon-like curses that the machines produced to attack Wishworks.

After that, she planned to use the curse-making machines to cook up some particularly nasty things to send to children on their birthdays. Nothing would give her greater pleasure than to watch an eager child open up a beautifully wrapped present only to find something awful inside of it. She had all kinds of ideas for unpleasant surprises: presents filled with cockroaches, rotten eggs, giant tarantulas, or stinky socks.

She couldn't help but grin as she walked down the spiral staircase that led to the dank workshop. Her Spider Monkey servants had been working around the clock to perfect her new invention. Finding the power source for her device had been the tricky part, and had required working with some dark and terrible creatures. But now that she possessed what she needed, she felt certain that her idea would work. All that remained was to test it.

As Penelope entered the sprawling workshop, a dozen Spider Monkeys wearing pink laboratory coats scuttled to attention.

Her invention was a crudely formed iron box attached to a pipe organ made from human bones: the remains of Thornblood's Curse-atina.[11]

Penelope's invention would have been immediately recognizable to anyone who had spent time in a busy city on Earth. Unfortunately, most of the Curseworks employees had never seen a parking meter before, and it had required several hours of explanation by Penelope to get them to understand the concept.

Penelope twisted the small knob that protruded underneath the parking meter's curved window.

"Somebody give me a quarter," Penelope said.

The nearest Spider Monkey smiled nervously, showing a row of exceptionally white teeth. "I'm sorry, Your Majesty, but the trolls reported very few of those in their last, er . . . extraction." He extended a shaky paw, revealing several

---

[11] The Curse-atina was Adolfus Thornblood's most famous invention: an instrument that, when played, produced terrible, dragonish curses. Only a few of Thornblood's original musical compositions are still around, and most music scholars agree that they required very little true musical talent to write. His self-proclaimed masterpiece was titled "Death, Death, Death to You, I Want To See You Die," sung to the tune of "Row, Row, Row Your Boat." Some evil scholars claim that it was Thornblood's gift with lyrics that made him a modern master, but others say that the evil President never had a music lesson in his life and really wasn't very good.

copper coins. "We do have these, though," he said hopefully.

"Pennies are too weak, you idiot!" Penelope's eyes flashed with rage. "They won't give us enough power. Get me something else!"

The scared Spider Monkey scuttled away to try to find a new coin. He returned a few minutes later holding a small, tarnished nickel in his hand.

"This is all we have besides pennies, Your Majesty. Snottrag, the miner's captain, said that they're working hard to steal more, but that it will take time."

Penelope snatched the nickel away and quickly put it in the meter's coin slot.

There was a small *click* followed by the sound of a timer ticking down. She watched as the glass window of the meter grew cloudy, filling with sickly green smoke. A terrible sound like fingernails on a chalkboard filled the air, and the Spider Monkey workers flinched and covered their ears. Penelope stared at the glass, eager to see what would happen next.

Soon, an image of a small girl holding a coin materialized. The girl made a wish, and then tossed the coin into a sparkling fountain.

The picture changed. The new image was of the girl's wish: a cute gray kitten with big blue eyes. The little cat crawled out of a wicker basket and into the smiling little girl's outstretched arms. She laughed excitedly as she petted the creature's soft, furry back.

Then, suddenly, the girl screamed. The kitten grew, changing into something terrible and monstrous. Its soft fur morphed into black, shiny scales. The sweet blue eyes bulged and turned a sickly, sulfurous yellow. It slowly turned its terrible gaze upon the girl and, instead of a kittenish mew, let out a horrible, screeching wail.

Penelope smiled. Her invention worked! She moved over to the pipe organ and placed her hands lightly on the finger-bone keys. She wondered what she should play. Would the machine produce curses if she played any kind of music, or did it have to be something evil?

Penelope launched into "The Witches' Dance," one of her favorite piano pieces. As she played, she heard a deep groan coming from inside the organ.

Moments later, a single twisting curl of green smoke appeared and morphed into a small, dragon-like creature.

The tiny creature flapped its leathery wings and darted around the ceiling, trying to escape the lab so it could travel down to Earth to deliver its curse. But because the lab had no windows, it couldn't find a way out. So, instead, it attacked several terrified Spider Monkeys by spitting out sizzling green acid.

Not bad, Penelope thought. It certainly wasn't the terrifying creature she had imagined, but it wasn't bad for a first try.

The meter clicked off. The winged dragon gave a small screech and vanished.

"Oh, well," Penelope muttered. "At least I got five minutes for a nickel. But twenty-five minutes for a quarter would be better." She turned to address her workers.

"You," she said, pointing at the white-toothed Spider Monkey. "Tell Snottrag and his trolls to go back into the tunnels. I need more coins! We've got to figure out how to make the curses last longer."

The Spider Monkey bowed and scuttled away. After watching him go, Penelope removed the thin, black leather book from her back pocket and flipped through the pages.

"Hey, Rottenbutt, do you know anybody who can translate Jinnish?"

Rottenjaw stared coldly at her before answering, "Why?"

Penelope shoved the book into his hands.

The adviser carefully examined the cover of the book. Then he flipped through the pages, studying them closely. "Only a Jinn could translate this book," he told her.

"Great. Where in the world are we going to get a Jinn to

help us? It's impossible!" Penelope scowled. Curseworks had never had any luck kidnapping a Jinn from Wishworks, and now that they had all fled the Factory, the odds were even worse of capturing one.

Rottenjaw removed his glasses and polished them with a pink handkerchief before replying smoothly, "Oh, I wouldn't say 'impossible,' Your Majesty."

Penelope looked up sharply. Rottenjaw replaced his glasses on his nose and looked down at her with hooded eyes.

"There's someone imprisoned beneath the Factory who can translate this perfectly."

≋ CHAPTER SEVEN ≋

The G.O.M.P.

"**N**OW!" Ben shouted. The group threw their Battlerangs. The weapons whizzed together through the air and collided with the monster's head.

"NO! NO! NO! Stop! You're hurting her!" A squeaky voice rose above the anguished cry of the metal monster. Ben and his friends grabbed their returning Battlerangs out of the air and stared at the sight that met their eyes.

Mounted on top of the mechanical monster, which looked like a huge gopher, was a gnome wearing bright green goggles. The gnome gestured wildly for Ben and the others to stop their Battlerang attack.

Ben held up his hand, signaling for everyone to stop. The gnome, who looked very relieved, leaped from his saddle and ran quickly over to the gopher's huge head, inspecting it for damage.

"My father's gonna kill me," Ben heard him mutter as he inspected the big dents left by the Battlerangs. The gopher purred and extended a metal tongue to lick the spot where it had been hurt.

"Why did you attack us?" the gnome demanded, removing his goggles.

"I, we, heard the roar and thought——" Ben started.

"You thought," the gnome fumed. "Well, if you had just *waited* two more seconds before you attacked us, I could have told you that her roar is only used to frighten the bats in these tunnels."

Nora, feeling defensive, stepped in front of Ben and poked a finger into the gnome's chest. Ben noticed that they were exactly the same height.

"How were we to know? We've never been down here before! Is this any way to welcome delegates from the Wishworks Factory?"

The gnome paused, his shaggy white eyebrows raised in surprise.

"You're from Wishworks?"

"Yes. I'm Nora O'Doyle. The assistant to the manager of Kids' Birthday Wishes Ages 3 to 12." The leprechaun puffed out her chest proudly. "And this is the manager himself, Benjamin Piff," she said, indicating Ben. Ben nodded, still shocked at the sight of the gnome and his mechanical pet.

"And this is Jeannie and Fizzle Fizzypop," Nora continued.

"You aren't related to Fulcrum Fizzypop,[12] are you?" the gnome whispered. "The greatest gum inventor who ever lived?"

Fizzle nodded. "Yeah, he's my grandpa. Why?"

The gnome's face broke into a wide, toothy grin. "Grease and gears! The granddaughter of Fulcrum Fizzypop right here in the Wishing Well Pipeline! Can I have your autograph?" he asked, pulling a grimy notepad and a stub of a pencil from his pocket.

Fizzle laughed and took the pencil. "I guess so."

The gnome looked delighted. After Fizzle signed his paper, he introduced himself to the group.

---

[12] Fulcrum Fizzypop's most famous gum, Swiftsneaker Citrus, could make the slowest-moving person run faster than a Feathered Funicula chair, filling them with boundless energy. The gum was hailed by lazy fairies everywhere as a national achievement.

"Geary Crankshaft, greatest of the Gnome inventors, at your service." He removed his tall pointed hat and bowed, his long braided beard almost touching the floor. Then he straightened and gestured to the metal creature behind him.

"And this beautiful creature is the G. O. M. P." The metal animal stopped licking its wounds long enough to raise its head and acknowledge the group.

"What's a Gomp?" Jeannie asked.

The gnome moved over to the creature's huge head and stroked it affectionately.

"G. - O. - M. - P. stands for Gopher Of Monstrous Proportions," he said proudly, kissing the animal on its shiny nose. "She's mine. And in case you've heard otherwise"—he looked suspiciously at the small group—"I built her myself without anybody's help."

Now it was Fizzle's turn to be impressed. She flitted over to the side of the gopher and stared at it with admiration.

"Impressive," she said, inspecting the rivets that held the large robot together. "It must have taken you forever to make. How does it work?"

"Well, uh . . ." Geary appeared to think hard for a moment before replying. "She . . . um . . . works on the principles of Infernal Dynamics, Perpetual Motivation, and . . . other stuff."

Ben noticed that the question seemed to have caught the gnome off guard.

"Wow," Fizzle said. She nodded, not seeming to notice. She appeared to be the only one in the group who understood what the gnome was talking about. "So then you must have applied Pherson Follop's theory of magical mechanics[13] to the power train?"

Geary hesitated for a split second before replying. Ben thought that it looked like he hadn't understood the question. Thinking quickly, the gnome pointed at the fairy and replied, "Yep, that's it. Bingo! You got it. Right on the money!"

Then, as if he wanted to quickly change the focus of the conversation, he said, "I assume that, being Fulcrum's granddaughter, you've done a bit of inventing yourself?"

Fizzle blushed. "Well, a little. I made a few twists and improvements on some of my grandpa's flavors. Right now I'm in the prototype phase of a brand-new kind of gum that can turn the chewer into all kinds of different animals. I'm calling it 'Zoo Chew' for now."

The gnome nodded slowly. "Interesting. Actually, one

---

[13] Pherson Follop's theory of magical mechanics is as follows: "If magic is put on something mechanical, then it will be turned into something magically mechanical." This theory was once hailed as a revolutionary new concept in the scientific community. Recently, however, many scholars have criticized Follop, claiming that he was merely stating the obvious.

of *my* greatest inventions can transform ordinary rocks into solid gold."

Ben, Nora, and Jeannie looked at Geary. They didn't believe a word he was saying.

"It's true," Geary continued. "My colleagues in the Gnomish science community were amazed that I had created such an incredible machine in only three days! Not to mention that I had done it at so young an age. But then again, I *was* born with an extraordinarily gifted mind."

"Wow! I have never heard of a *mechanical* transformer," Fizzle gushed. "I thought transformations could only be accomplished with fairy magic. You've got to tell me how it works."

Ben snorted. The arrogant gnome was getting on his nerves. Why did it seem like everyone but Fizzle could see that the guy was a total fake?

"Um, I'm sorry to interrupt," Ben said to Fizzle, cutting off Geary's bragging. "But we kind of have a problem here. We've got to figure out how to get the helmet out of the water, remember?"

"Oh, sorry, Ben," Fizzle said, giving Geary a wink. "Guess we were getting carried away."

Geary turned to Ben and asked, "What helmet?"

Ben filled Geary in on their mission and the helmet.

Geary listened attentively and seemed especially interested when Ben described what the helmet looked like. After asking Ben several specific questions about the numerous gears and switches on the helmet, Geary exclaimed, "Cogs and crankshafts! I wonder if it's the same helmet that we studied in my Mechanical Marvels class at school. It sounds just like the Clockwork Helmet that Togglenoggin the Fourth gave to President Thicklepick after the First Wishworks War!"[14]

The gnome strode briskly over to the G. O. M. P.

"Don't worry. I'll have it out of there no time." He put his goggles back on and swung himself into the G. O. M. P.'s saddle. "Stand back, everybody."

The group backed up against the cavern walls to get out of the way. Geary pushed several buttons and knobs on the gopher's back and then pulled back on a big ratcheting lever.

HUMMMMMMMMMM! Ben felt the little hairs on his arms rise as a tingle of magnetic power filled the air. He glanced over at the deep pool of black water beneath the bucket. The water rippled in response to the beam of invisible energy

---

[14] One of the most famous Gnomish regiments in the First Wishworks War was called "The Fighting Gremlins," led by Pingpong Bottlerocket. They were highly decorated for their speedy repairs of the Battle Chairs after they had been shot down by Abul Cadabra's Jinn army.

that was radiating out of the mechanical gopher.

Seconds later, tiny splashes like little jumping fish filled the entire surface of the dark pool. Ben watched as coins shot out of the water and landed in the G. O. M. P.'s mouth.

"It's collecting all of the coins that were thrown into the Wishing Well," Ben said, figuring out what was happening.

After several moments of collecting coins, a big splash echoed in the cavern. The lost helmet flew from the bottom of the well and clanked into the G. O. M. P.'s waiting jaws.

"Got it!" Geary shouted as he threw the switch that cut off the gopher's magnetic field.

"Wow, thanks!" Ben said, rushing to get the helmet.

"No problem," Geary said. Fizzle flew up and planted a friendly kiss on the gnome's bulbous nose, making him blush a deeper shade of red.

"Ahem." Geary cleared his throat. "Well, I, um, suppose I should take you all to see the king. He'll be anxious to find out about your mission."

"That'd be great, thanks." Ben was feeling a bit jealous over the attention Geary had gotten from Fizzle. He was surprised at how much her connection with the gnome bothered him.

As they followed the clanking G. O. M. P. down the side passageway, Ben's resentful feelings must have shown, because Jeannie floated up next to him and gave him a curious look.

"Jealous?" she asked.

"What? No way," Ben said, trying to act casual. "That guy is probably four hundred years old."

"Well, Fizzle's almost a hundred and twenty in fairy years. And besides, gnomes are born looking old. Most boys lose their hair and have beards by the time they turn ten. I'll bet he's only a few years older than you are."[15]

"Well, how old are *you?*" Ben asked Jeannie.

She smiled prettily at him. "You wouldn't believe me if I told you."

"Try me," Ben said.

"Three thousand," she said, giving him a wink.

"What? Really?" Ben said, shocked. Jeannie chuckled and elbowed him playfully. "Not really. I'm only thirteen."

Ben felt was relieved. If Jeannie had really been that old, he would have felt like he should be wearing diapers!

---

[15] In the Gnomish world, it is a significant right of passage when a ten-year-old boy grows his first beard. A party, called a Beard-Mitzvah is held for the youngster, and he is granted a special wish from the Wishworks Factory. A similar party is held for girls, but fortunately, they don't have to grow beards to have it.

She smiled at Ben and said, "If I was three thousand, I'd be able to use the really powerful magic."

"Really?" Ben asked, wanting to know more.

"Yeah, Jinns get more magic power the older they get. Right now, I can only do the basic things like fly and change shape. After my eighteenth birthday, I'll have wish-granting power and the ability to use magic as a weapon. Until then, I'm stuck using these to defend myself." She glanced down at the Battlerang that was hooked on her belt.[16]

As Ben and Jeannie chatted and walked down the twisting passages, Ben was amazed at how comfortable he was feeling around her. She had definitely surprised him with her change in attitude.

They were so busy talking that at one point Ben almost stepped on Nora, who was walking in front of them.

"Hey, watch it!" she said, glaring up at Ben. Ben was surprised by her reaction. He had never seen her so upset over a simple accident.

"Sorry. I didn't see you," he said.

"Well if you weren't so busy talking to *her*, maybe you'd be more careful of where you were walking!" Nora shot

---

[16] Most Jinns prefer using curved swords to defend themselves and only use Battlerangs when absolutely necessary.

Jeannie an icy stare. Jeannie moved forward, floating up next to Ben.

"He said he was sorry," the Jinn said, glaring back at Nora. "Besides, he couldn't help it if he couldn't see you. It's not like he brought along a magnifying glass or anything."

Ben saw the leprechaun's face turn bright red at the insult. *Uh-oh.* He could tell that Nora was really angry.

"Trolls!" Geary whispered, suddenly cutting off the girls' argument. He began frantically punching buttons on the G. O. M. P.'s control panel. "And I think there are a lot of 'em." He turned backward in his saddle and glanced at Ben. "Get those weapons of yours ready. We're gonna need all the firepower we've got!"

CHAPTER EIGHT

The Half Jinn

Penelope looked apprehensively at the heavy black door that led to the prisoner's cell. Rottenjaw unlocked the door and pushed it open. Penelope gasped when she saw what was inside. A creature with a wispy tail of gray smoke lay huddled in the corner. She tried to look away but couldn't.

"I refuse to be hooked up to that machine again," the creature said. "You promised to set me free after the last time."

"Yes, yes. All in good time," Rottenjaw replied smoothly.

"But today I've brought you a visitor." Rottenjaw indicated Penelope with a sweep of his delicately gloved hand.

"What machine is he talking about?" Penelope asked.

"The machine that powers the Factory, of course," Rottenjaw replied. "We have been using this *creature* to generate the Factory's power. Believe it or not, this pathetic thing lying here has kept Curseworks from falling apart." Rottenjaw stared disdainfully at the bundle of rags. "But it couldn't generate a single curse."

"Why didn't you tell me about this sooner? I didn't know we had a Jinn at Curseworks!" Penelope looked angry.

"Well, not exactly a *Jinn*," Rottenjaw said, trying to calm down Penelope. "It's only a *Half Jinn*. A 'Halfer,' as the full-blooded Jinns like to call such creatures. It only possesses a small amount of magic."[17]

Part of the blanket that covered the creature's face fell away, and Penelope screamed. Half of the Jinn's face looked like handsome human boy of around fifteen. The other half was a crumpled mass of misshapen gray flesh.

The Jinn could tell that Penelope was repulsed by his appearance, so he quickly turned the disfigured side of his

---

[17] Because of the unpopularity of Half Jinns, not much is recorded about their specific magical talents. Some scholars on Jinnish culture believe that Half Jinns might have powers that are as yet undiscovered.

face away from her searching eyes.

"Here," Penelope said, tossing the book at the creature. "See if you can translate this for me."

The Jinn didn't move immediately.

"Move when the president of Curseworks commands you, fool!" Rottenjaw commanded, kicking the Half Jinn in his ribs.

The Jinn winced. He obediently picked up the book and turned to the page that Penelope had flagged.

"Well, can you tell me what's there or not?" Penelope demanded, growing impatient.

"Yes, Mistress, I can." He stared at Penelope with his bright blue eyes.

The thought that the Half Jinn had very pretty eyes in spite of the ugly side of his face flitted through Penelope's mind, but she forced it back down.

"Well then, do it. I haven't got all day!" she said impatiently.

The boy nodded and began to read.

> *"The words of Al'Kazaam, faithful servant of his Imperial Majesty Abul Cadabra, Greatest of Jinns, to the Chosen Two:*

"Seek fire and water, wind and stone,
Secret locks and Key of Bone;
There four deaths await the unworthy soul,
Who seeks to travel the paths below.

"The first in the roots of cursed tree,
The second awash in boiling seas;
The third, the howl of tortured stone,
The fourth will burn in fires cold.

"Of mortal flesh, the Cursed Jinn,
And Enemies' Daughter shall venture in;
There they'll see their heart's desire:
My Master's Lamp dwells in the fire."

Penelope stared at the Half Jinn for a long moment after he finished reading. It looked as though he understood some part of the puzzling rhyme.

Penelope turned to Rottenjaw and said excitedly, "This is exactly what I've been looking for! With the Lamp of One Thousand Nightmares, I'll be able to completely destroy my cousin and his stupid Wishworks Factory. And not only that"—her eyes narrowed craftily—"when I command Abul Cadabra, all the Jinns that Curseworks could ever want will come rushing to our doors. Then the real fun will begin."

Rottenjaw nodded slowly, trying as hard as he could to keep his excitement contained behind a mask-like expression. This was fantastic news!

"Leave us," Penelope commanded. "I want to be alone with him."

Rottenjaw raised his eyebrows in surprise. "But, Your Majesty, I can see no reason to—"

"I said get out of here, okay, Rottenbutt?" Penelope shot her adviser an irritated glance. "I want to talk to him alone."

Rottenjaw inclined his head and exited the room, gently closing the heavy door behind him.

As Rottenjaw ascended the winding stone staircase, he heard the patter of small footsteps in the corridor above. When he reached the top stair, a small figure clothed in a patchy pink suit and a bowler hat was waiting for him.

"Well?" the grizzled leprechaun said.

Rottenjaw shot Paddy O'Doyle a satisfied look. "She's found the secret to Abul Cadabra's Lamp." He pulled at the fingertips of his pink gloves, sliding them off of his delicate hands. "It won't be long before she sets off to go find it."

Paddy scratched his stubbly cheek. "I don't get it. Why are you letting her go get it? Seems to me like we should grab it for ourselves—"

Rottenjaw interrupted, "The legends say that the lamp is guarded by dark and terrible powers. Things so awful that even books are afraid to mention exactly what they're capable of doing." Rottenjaw shuddered involuntarily. "But, if by some miracle, the girl succeeds and returns with the lamp, then, Mr. O'Doyle, we'll simply arrange for an unfortunate 'accident' to take Miss Piff out of our way."

He paused to polish the lenses of his tiny spectacles. Then he glanced down at his pink cloak, tie, and vest and grimaced. "And one of the first things *I'm* going to do as Curseworks' newest president is to get rid of these *ridiculous* clothes."

≥ Chapter Nine ≥

The Trolls

*C*LANG! Ben ducked just in time to avoid the pickax that crashed into the stony wall above his head. The beefy-looking troll who had swung it croaked with laughter, the kerosene lamp that was affixed to his mining helmet bobbed up and down, casting an eerie shadow on his long, gnarled face. Ben noticed with horror that the troll had glowing red pinpricks for eyes.

"Get back!" Ben yelled. The troll was much too close for Ben to throw his Battlerang, so he swung it around, hoping to drive the creature away.

"GAHHHRRR!" the creature howled, trying to avoid the sharp-edged Battlerang.

Just a few steps more, Ben thought desperately. As soon as the troll was far enough away, he cocked his arm back and threw his Battlerang with all of his might.

The weapon whistled through the air, glowing with searing white fire. The shot was well aimed and struck the troll right between the eyes.

Bull's-eye!

Jeannie, Fizzle, and Nora were fighting off trolls, too. The defeated trolls were piling up all around them.

More trolls descended upon Ben. With an incredible bank shot, he knocked two of them down at once. Seeing this, the rest of the trolls panicked and fled down a side passage, their angry howls echoing in the darkness.

Ben wearily grabbed his returning Battlerang. After slipping it into his back pocket, he wiped a shaking hand across his sweaty forehead.

"Is everyone okay?" he asked.

Jeannie, Fizzle, and Nora all nodded. Ben noticed that their faces were pale and seemed a bit frightened.

Ben glanced over to check on Geary. The gnome was bending over the left foreleg of his mechanical G. O. M. P. and muttering to himself. Ben could see that a piece of the gopher's leg had been punctured by a pickax.

"No, no, no. My father will kill me! This is really, really bad," the gnome fretted.

Ben glanced at Nora, hoping she'd know what to do. She shrugged and shook her head.

"Hey, Geary," Ben said as gently as he could. The gnome's face was pale, and his hands were shaking.

"He'll never forgive me . . . can't fix it in time . . . I never should have taken it out of the garage."

Fizzle flitted over and placed a tiny hand on Geary's shoulder. She whispered soothingly to him as Ben backed away.

"I don't get it," Ben said, scratching his head under the brim of his hat. "It's only a puncture in the metal. If he built the thing, can't he fix it when we get to Tiktokket?"

"I think there might be something more going on here," said Jeannie, floating over to Ben. "I heard him mention his father when we first met him in the cavern. I have a feeling that our little friend here took his dad's car keys without permission, if you know what I mean?"

Ben suddenly realized what the Jinn was hinting at. Geary was acting just like a kid with a new driver's license who had taken his father's car without permission and put a big dent in it. The gnome had probably made up the whole thing about how he had invented the G. O. M. P. just to impress them.

"Hey, listen," Ben said, walking back over to Geary. He felt sorry for the gnome now. "When we get to Tiktokket, we'll tell your dad that it was our fault, that you were just trying to protect us from the trolls, okay?"

Geary wiped the corner of his eye with one of the braids of his long beard and glanced up at Ben. "Would you really do that?" he asked in a quiet voice.

"Sure," Ben said with a smile. "If we explain the whole thing, I'm sure he'll totally understand."

Geary sighed. "I doubt it. You don't know my father. The G. O. M. P. is his favorite invention." The gnome straightened up and extended a gnarled little hand for Ben to shake. "But it's really nice of you to offer. Thanks."

Ben grinned and shook his hand.

A few moments later they were moving back down the tunnel. The G. O. M. P. could walk, but it was moving slower than before.

I wonder what his dad is like? Ben thought as they plodded down the passageway.

They had been walking by the soft glow of Fizzle's fairy light for about a mile when the tunnel suddenly began to grow brighter. A few moments later, they rounded a corner and saw the source of the light.

Ben's jaw dropped as he saw the incredible brass city of Tiktokket stretched out in front of him. The Gnomish city was made entirely out of whirring and whizzing mechanical inventions. Ben was amazed at the twittering birds flying through the air and the huge, ticking metal trees with slowly revolving leaves. And growing from the trees were small metal picnic baskets!

One had fallen to the ground, and Ben picked it up. Glancing inside, he was delighted to find a small metal thermos filled with hot chocolate, and three sweet, gear-shaped cakes.

"Hey, check it out!" Ben called to his friends. But before anyone had a chance to respond, Geary spoke up.

"Get ready, everyone," he said. "Here come my father's guards."

Chapter Ten

The Diplomatic Mission

"*I*'ve figured out how just about everything on this ship works except for one weird thing in the engine compartment." Jonathan Pickles blew a strand of shaggy brown hair out of his eyes. He was sitting in front of the control panel of the Cornucopia, a flying submarine that was also one of the four weapons of incredible power.

Candlewick had instructed Ben's friends Jonathan and Gene to get the sub ready for a trip to the Jinn Territories. Jonathan, who was gifted with mechanics, had helped to revive the vehicle during the last Wishworks War. Gene, a hulking Jinn and one of Jonathan's close friends, was the best pilot that the Factory had seen in years, and one of the few who had figured out how to fly the magical machine.

"What's the thing you can't figure out?" Gene asked. The big purple Jinn floated up to the cockpit and hovered next to Jonathan.

"It looks like a big heart-shaped hole. It's almost as if there's a piece missing," Jonathan said. He hated a problem that he couldn't solve. It was one of the reasons he was such a great a technician at the Thaumaturgic Cardioscope.

"I was reading through the manuals again last night, but I couldn't find anything about it. It's driving me crazy," Jonathan said.

"Hmm, that is strange," Gene mused. "But at least we don't need the missing piece to fly the Cornucopia. I've never gotten to pilot a more amazing machine."

"What part is missing?" Candlewick's lanky frame descended through the Cornucopia's hatch and into the luxurious cabin.

"Jonathan says that there's a heart-shaped chamber in the engine that has a missing part. Do you know anything about it?"

Candlewick shook his head. "No, can't say that I do. Does it present any mechanical problems?"

Jonathan shrugged. "No, it seems to run okay without it. I just finished a final check on all the systems two hours ago. Everything's great," he said.

"Good." Candlewick looked anxious. "Boys, this is a very important trip. It might be the last chance we have to come to a peaceful arrangement with the Jinns."

"Are you meeting with my father?" Gene asked, his expression suddenly grave. The Jinn's father was head of the Jinnish Labor Union and had been the one to initiate the walkout from Wishworks.

"Yes. It took a lot of doing, but he finally agreed."

Gene shrugged and turned back to the controls. "My dad and I haven't spoken since I became friends with Ben. If you can get through to him, then be my guest."

Candlewick and Jonathan exchanged glances. They could both tell that the topic of Gene's father was a sore point.

"Well, let's get going, then," Candlewick said, changing the subject. "The sooner we get there, the sooner we can put an end to this misunderstanding."

Candlewick handed Gene his magical pocket watch, which worked as a key to the flying machine. The Jinn carefully placed it into a recessed spot on the dashboard.

VROOOOOM! The massive engines of the beautiful, winged submarine roared in response. Moments later, she was ascending into the air, forcing huge gusts of wind downward from her long flapping wings.

As Candlewick settled back into a red velvet chair, he glanced out of the brass porthole at the rapidly descending Factory below. He was nervous about the upcoming negotiations. Too much was at stake.

His eyes traveled down to his leather briefcase and the contract inside. The new incentives he'd come up with included massive shares of Wishworks stock for every Jinnish employee and a very serious penalty for any human imprisoning a Jinn in a lamp. It was the first time in history that Wishworks had ever put such a thing in writing.[18]

Candlewick sighed. They desperately needed the Jinns, help to rebuild Wishworks and fortify its defenses in case Curseworks decided to launch another attack. Not only that, but there were countless wishes that were going unanswered due to the shorthanded supply of wish-granting magic.

It had better work, he thought determinedly.

Candlewick glanced over at the two boys. Gene was maneuvering the controls; Jonathan was sitting in the

---

[18] Breaking a written contract with a Jinn is the most dangerous of offenses. Jinnish law states that the penalty for the offender is to be covered in honey and almonds and then tossed out to the Sand Dragons that live in the J'uhst Desert. People eaten by Sand Dragons are slowly and painfully digested by the monsters for over a thousand years.

copilot's chair. Both boys looked surprisingly relaxed and happy.

I'm glad they have no idea how much danger we're about to get into, Candlewick thought grimly. *It's better not to tell them yet.*

◎ ◎ ◎

From Candlewick's office in the highest tower in the Wishworks Factory, a beautiful woman with brown eyes watched the submarine fly away until it was only a tiny speck in the distance.

"Good luck, Thom," Delores whispered. She was Thomas Candlewick's newly appointed assistant. Perkins, Candlewick's previous assistant, had served faithfully for many years in that position before his death in the last Wishworks War.

The pretty brunette's face was full of concern. She and Candlewick had grown very close over the last few months. She thought about the romantic dinner they'd had the night before at the newly refurbished Pot o' Gold restaurant and sighed.

Delores sat down at her desk and tried not to worry. She knew the mission Candlewick was on was very dangerous.

"Please bring him back," she murmured quietly. "I don't want to lose him."

≋ CHAPTER ELEVEN ≋
Penelope and Preztoe

"So I take it your name is Gene, right?" Penelope said, leaning against the rough dungeon wall.

"As a matter of fact, no. My given name is Preztoe," replied the Half Jinn coolly, trying to keep the ugly side of his face hidden.

Penelope was intrigued. She had been told during her days at Wishworks that Jinns never revealed their real names. Supposedly, to know a Jinn's given name was to give the person who knew it power over the Jinn. Only family or married couples used the real names.

"I don't get it. Why would you tell me that?" Penelope asked, her eyes narrowed with suspicion. "I hardly know you."

"Because the standard rules don't apply to me. I am half Jinn and half human. Knowing my name makes no difference."

Penelope didn't want to admit to herself that she found the boy interesting. She would never, ever say it aloud, but there was something about him that she actually liked.

"I saw the look on your face when you translated that rhyme. You know something, don't you?"

Preztoe studied her for a long time before replying. "I do."

Penelope eased herself into a sitting position and moved, ever so slightly, toward the Half Jinn.

"Then tell me. What is it you know?"

Preztoe shrugged. "Until now, I had only heard the second half of that rhyme. I learned it as a small child. My mother was human, and I never knew my father . . ." The boy paused a moment, as if reminded of a painful memory. "She tried to hide me from the other, normal Jinns until I was four years old. She used to sing the song to me while I was locked in my room. She made me memorize it. That was all before . . ." His voice trailed off, and he lowered his gaze.

". . . The other Jinns found you and forced you to leave," Penelope finished.

The Half Jinn nodded.

Normally, stories about other people's problems annoyed Penelope. She found most people to be much less interesting than herself. However, there was something about Preztoe's situation that she could understand. She knew what it was like not to be wanted. Her parents had never wanted her. In fact, she was sure they hadn't even noticed she was gone.

"So, what was the song she sung to you?" she asked, ready to change the subject.

The Jinn smiled. "It went like this." He closed his eyes and began to sing softly.

> *"Touch not the pools, O Enemies' Daughter,*
> *And look not long into the water;*
> *For she'll inherit the half man's fate,*
> *And halves made whole, one day shall mate.*
>
> *"The seventh son born of that marriage,*
> *Will undo all and earn disparage;*
> *From he who sleeps at the World's core,*
> *This much I'll say and will say no more.*

"But follow my words and finish the quest,
Bring back the lamp at my behest;
And unlimited power will be your reward,
Terrible wrath and swiftest sword.

"Heed these words of Al'Kazaam
O son of Jinn and mortal man."

"You can see why she sang it to me," Preztoe said when he was done. "It's probably the only song in Jinnish that ever mentions a *Halfer*."

Penelope's mind raced. The rhyme was very confusing, but it hinted at great and terrible power for the one who found the Lamp of One Thousand Nightmares and brought Abul Cadabra back to life.

Turning to Preztoe, she said eagerly, "The trolls have been tunneling deep in the mines. I made sure that they would report back to me if they found anything interesting. They found this in one of the passageways."

She took a strangely designed key from her jeans pocket and handed it to Preztoe.

The Half Jinn turned the key over in his hand. The key had a skull-shaped handle and looked like it was made from human bones.

"I'm not sure what this key could be for," Preztoe said.

"Translate that very first part of the poem again," Penelope demanded, shoving the book in front him.

Preztoe took it and read, "*Seek fire and water, wind and stone—*"

Penelope interrupted. "No, no, no. The second line," she said impatiently.

"*Secret locks and Key of Bone . . .*"

"That's it!" she exclaimed. "The key is made of bones. I'll bet it opens the secret locks!"

"What secret locks?" Preztoe asked.

"I'm not sure, but I bet it has something to do with Abul Cadabra's Lamp of One Thousand Nightmares. Come on. We have no time to lose. I've got to get my hands on that lamp!"

In her excitement, she seized Preztoe by the arm and tried to help him stand. But the Half Jinn was very weak and had a hard time hovering on his wispy cloud of smoke. He crashed against the wall, exposing the horrible side of his face to Penelope. She cringed when she saw it, but not quite as much as before.

"What's the matter?"

"Can't move," the Half Jinn stated, his chest heaving. "Haven't . . . eaten . . . in days."

Penelope watched as the strain overcame him and he collapsed to the floor.

"Okay, wait here. I'll get you some food, and then we'll go," she said hurriedly as she dashed through the heavy oak door. Then, with a second thought, she poked her head back inside and said with a scowl, "Don't even think of escaping while I'm gone."

Preztoe shrugged feebly and said sarcastically, "Yeah, right. Where would I go?"

Feeling satisfied with the answer, Penelope dashed up the winding staircase to the Curseworks kitchen. She passed two of her Horrible Snifter guards, who saluted her, their thin white fingers snapping upward to their tall, furry pink hats. She nodded at them and continued on. As the familiar foul stench of the Curseworks kitchen reached her nostrils, she realized that she was quietly singing a verse from the song that Preztoe had been singing a few moments ago.

> *"Touch not the pools, O Enemies' Daughter,*
> *And look not long into the water;*
> *For she'll inherit the half man's fate,*
> *And halves made whole, one day shall mate."*

CHAPTER TWELVE

King Togglenoggin

"Trolls! Blasted, dirty trolls!" the Gnome king sputtered.

Ben thought that the little round king was going to explode. He was by far the smallest gnome that he'd seen since entering Tiktokket. His tall crown was covered with ticking gears that contained huge rubies, which glittered as they slowly revolved. Standing at attention next to his throne were two tall, thin gnomes. These royal attendants wore tall hats that looked like smokestacks.

King Togglenoggin took a drink of mineral water.[19] After gulping a huge quantity, he seemed to calm down.

"In the last week, the trolls have raided over one hundred wells in the Pipeline. Not since the time of my father, Bunsen Togglenoggin the Fourth, has there been such a disaster!"

"Wait a sec. Do you mean they're taking the coins?" Ben asked, alarmed. "What's happening to all the wishes that are attached to them?"

The king sighed. "We don't know. The trolls never showed any interest at all in the coins until recently. We haven't sent a single shipment to Wishworks all week!" The king held his large head in his hands and moaned.

"I promise that we'll help you get those coins back," Ben told the king. "There's no way we can let the trolls get away with stealing all those wishes."

"Does Candlewick know about the missing coins?" the king asked worriedly. "Is that why he sent you down here?"

Ben shook his head. "We're here to find the weapons the Gnomes helped the Factory build during the First Wishworks War." Ben handed the Clockwork Helmet to the

---

[19] Mineral water is the favorite Gnomish drink. It is said to make the men's beards grow longer and make the women's hair turn curly and sprout silver flowers. It also contains the vitamins A, B, C, D, L, P, R, Z, and the ever-popular mineral, Purple Zot 5.

king. "Candlewick thought that this might be a clue to help us get the Thaumaphor. Do you know anything about it?"

The king looked at the helmet and sighed. "This helmet is well known to us. But how it works remains a mystery. My father gave it to President Thicklepick as a gift. Many of our greatest scientific minds have tried to figure out its secret, but all have failed."

"I don't understand. Didn't the Gnomes make the helmet?" Ben asked.

The king grimaced. "The gnome who created the Clockwork Helmet was Beaker Blastingcapp.[20] He was very proud of his invention and never told anyone how he had made it. Later, he was sent on a mission to hide the Thaumaphor and witnessed terrible things along the way. He was the only one of his traveling companions who survived. And when he came back, he was totally insane."

King Togglenoggin shrugged helplessly. "All that anyone could get out of Blastingcapp before he died was that the Thaumaphor is hidden in a place so terrible and dangerous

---

[20] "The Ballad of Beaker Blastingcapp" is well known to the gnomes of Tiktokket and is often sung as a "working song" in many of the research laboratories. Unfortunately, it is usually accompanied by the sound of many hammers banging on metal parts, and the words and melody are almost impossible to make out above the clanging din.

that no gnome should ever dare look for it."

"But what about the inscription in the helmet? Most of the words are pretty worn, but Candlewick thought it said 'Seek the 4 Elements. Use with caution to find where the Thaumaphor is kept,' " Ben said.

The king shook his head, and his beard waggled. "No. The inscription was written by Beaker Blastingcapp when he first returned from the mission. It says: 'See the 4 Elementals. Use with caution. Thaumaphor is kept safe.' "

"But what are the four Elementals? Is that some kind of clue?" Ben asked the Gnome king.

"During one of Blastingcapp's insane mutterings, he mentioned that there were four Elementals: mythical creatures that guarded the spot where he hid the Thaumaphor."

"But that's impossible. The Elementals aren't real!" Nora blurted out. "My parents told me so when I was little. I used to be so scared of them that I couldn't sleep."

"She's right," Jeannie added. "I was told the same stories. The Elementals were evil creatures that had the power of Fire, Earth, Water, and Air and could destroy anyone who tried to fight them." The girl looked nervous. "But they were just stories made up to frighten little kids, right?"

Ben noticed that both Jeannie and Nora looked pale.

The king shrugged. "I don't know. All I can tell you is what we could figure out from Blastingcapp's insane mutterings."

"Well, whether they are real or not, we have to find the Thaumaphor," Ben concluded. "Do you have any record of where Beaker Blastingcapp began his journey?"

The king nodded and snapped his tiny fingers, sending one of his guards scurrying from the throne room. Moments later, the guard returned bearing a small leather book.

"This is the journal that he kept when he went on the expedition. It contains a map." He handed it to Ben, who accepted the journal gratefully.

"We discovered a tunnel not far from here that was dug by the trolls. It should intersect the part of the Pipeline where Blastingcapp set off on his quest. Hopefully during your search for the Thaumaphor, you can discover what the trolls are doing with the Wishing Well coins."

"We'll do our best," Ben said, stowing Beaker Blastingcapp's journal in his coat pocket.

Up until this moment, the king had taken no notice of Geary Crankshaft. The young gnome had hoped that with all of the other discussions about trolls and the four weapons, he would be forgotten. But to his dismay, the king now leveled his gaze directly at him, and his expression was anything but friendly.

"Geary Crankshaft, step forward."

Nora, who was standing next to the visibly frightened gnome, gave his arm an encouraging squeeze.

"Yes, Father, I . . . I . . . mean . . . Y-Your Majesty?" the gnome stammered.

The king continued, sounding exasperated. "Once again you have defied me. I told you that you were not allowed to use the G. O. M. P. and that you were to be confined to your quarters in the palace."

Geary hung his head.

"That invention was priceless! Now they tell me that one of its legs was destroyed!"

"Excuse me, Your Majesty," Ben interrupted, stepping forward. "I don't mean to intrude on, um, family business or anything. But I just wanted to let you know that Geary really helped us out when we were attacked back there. Also, if it hadn't been for his G. O. M. P., I don't know if we ever could have recovered the Clockwork Helmet. It dropped to the bottom of the well and we didn't think that we would ever get it back."

"*His* G. O. M. P.?" the king roared at Ben's statement. The cavern was suddenly filled with dark mutterings from the assembled scientists. "Do you mean to tell me that he took credit for inventing the G. O. M. P.?" King Togglenoggin's eyes flashed dangerously. Apparently, Geary's lie about having created the mechanical gopher was a really big deal to the gnomes.

"But, Father, I didn't——" Geary started desperately.

"DON'T CALL ME FATHER!" the king shouted back. "You have not earned the right to be called a Togglenoggin. You're a disgrace to all Gnomekind!"

Geary's face turned bright red.

Ben felt awful. He didn't mean to blurt out that Geary had taken credit for inventing the G. O. M. P.

"Taking credit for another gnome's work is the most serious of offenses. It's only made worse by the shameful fact that you have never even invented a single useful machine by yourself! Why, by the time I was your age, I already had over forty-four to my name!

"Take him to the Barbershop!" the king shouted.

"FATHER, NO!" Geary cried. "Please, no! Not that. I'll do anything. Please!"

Ben looked from father to son, confused. What was so bad about going to the Barbershop? From the way the gnomes were reacting, it must be something terrible.

The king pretended not to hear him as he sat on his throne. Moments later, a grim-looking gnome wearing a red-and-white-striped lab coat and holding a pair of scissors appeared. The king ignored Geary's renewed protests and motioned for the guards to lead him away.

After Geary had been led from the throne room, Ben broke the tense silence.

"What . . . what will happen to him, Your Majesty?"

The king shot Ben a hard look.

"If it's okay to ask, that is," Ben added humbly.

"He will be given a shave and a haircut," said the king flatly.

The gnomes in the room gasped at the pronouncement. The king held up his tiny hand for silence.

"Until Geary proves himself worthy of being called a true inventor, he is no longer my son."

CHAPTER THIRTEEN

Kumahumato

"Oh, Mahdi, how could you?" Mahdi's father's eyes were filled with disappointment.

"But Father, I made a wish—" Mahdi began.

"A wish isn't going to help us. I trusted you to bring home food and water!"

Mahdi wanted to speak, to tell his father that they would have all the water they would ever need when his wish came true. But his father wasn't listening. Mahdi knew that it was pointless to try to convince him that what he had done wasn't foolish.

The flies buzzed about Mahdi's head as he walked over to his favorite acacia tree. Sitting down in the shade was not much cooler than being out in the sun, but Mahdi sat there, anyway, and drew pictures with his finger in the dusty earth.

"When my wish comes true, he will forgive me," Mahdi said quietly as he wiped the dust from his finger and looked up into the branches of the ancient tree. "Then everything will be all right."

≋ CHAPTER FOURTEEN ≋

Unknown Fears

"**I**'m not going. I don't care what you say—I just can't do it!"

Ben had never seen Nora so afraid before. The little leprechaun's face was pale, and her eyes darted nervously around the restaurant, as if she were looking for the nearest exit. She hadn't touched any of the food that the clockwork chefs at Ticky Tock's Chocolate Shop had prepared.

Ben scooped up a delicious bite of "melting gear," a cake made in the shape of a gear, with warm, melted chocolate and caramel in the center.

"Mmm," he said, swallowing. "I don't get it. What's so bad about these Elemental guys, anyway? We've faced worse, haven't we? What about Penelope's Horrible Snifters?"

"This is different, Ben," Jeannie said. The Jinnish girl hadn't ordered anything off the menu, and had been sitting quietly with her arms folded protectively around her. "These *guys*, as you called them, are in the scariest stories told by the magical peoples. They're really awful."

"But what are they?" Ben asked. "Are they monsters made out of Earth, Air, Fire, and Water, or what?"

"The story I heard was that Abul Cadabra created them."

As soon as Jeannie mentioned the evil Jinn's name, Nora jumped, nearly knocking over Ben's glass of mineral water.

"Hey! Careful!" he said, steadying the glass. Nora whimpered an apology and hid her face behind her hands. Fizzle, who didn't seem to be as traumatized as the other girls, stopped eating her own chocolate gear and laid a comforting hand on Nora's shoulder.

"And how does the story go after that?" Ben asked, turning his attention back to Jeannie.

She shrugged nervously and continued. "Cadabra kidnapped one of each of the four magical races: a leprechaun, a gnome, a Jinn, and a fairy. The leprechauns have always lived near the water, and the gnomes live in the earth. Jinns have hearts that are made from blue fire, and the fairies are born to float through the air. The legends say that Cadabra used magic from each of them and transformed them into the Elementals."

"And that he created the Elementals to use against humans, whom he hated. He wanted to use the Elementals to wipe humans off the face of the Wishing World,"[21] Nora added.

"Abul Cadabra used the darkest magic to create them," Jeannie said, trying to remain calm. "Really evil stuff. They're supposed to be almost impossible to destroy. Some of the stories say that they can turn invisible and sneak up behind you to attack."

"Yeah, and I heard that if they ever catch you, the first thing they do is take your eyes!" Nora squeaked.

"Those stories sound like vampire tales I've heard," Ben commented. "Maybe we should bring along a wooden stake and some garlic," he joked.

"I don't know what a 'vampire' is," said Fizzle. "But

---

[21] Many scary stories told to youngsters involve Abul Cadabra's hatred of all living things, especially humans. Some of the smarter leprechauns have argued this point, asking the intelligent question, "If he hates all living things, and he's alive, then why doesn't he destroy himself?" The answer to this is a mystery.

wouldn't you feel scared if you found out it was real?"

Ben shrugged and took his last bite of cake. "Yeah, I guess so. But after some of the crazy things I've seen since I've been up here, I don't think that would scare me now."

Standing up, Ben offered to pay the check for the desserts they'd eaten, but Sabrina Stickshift, the gnome who owned the restaurant, refused, claiming that it was an honor to have such great adventurers at her shop.

As they left the restaurant and walked down streets lined with buildings that ticked and turned with gears and clockwork decorations, Ben tried to persuade Nora to change her mind about abandoning the mission. He walked beside her, begging her to stay and promising that he would look after her and protect her from the Elementals.

When he said this last part, Nora snorted softly.

"Yeah, right. I should be the one looking after you," she said quietly. She looked up into Ben's eyes. "That's supposed to be my job, isn't it?"

Ben knelt beside her, his brown eyes looking intently into her green ones.

"C'mon, Nora, please. I can't do this without you."

The leprechaun gazed back at Ben and blushed. After an awkward moment, Ben reached over and gave her a half hug. She grinned and gave him a little punch on the arm.

"All I can say is that I'm crazy for letting you talk me into this."

Ben grinned back at her. "You'll see," he said. "Everything will work out fine." He turned to the others. "There's always hope."

⪦ CHAPTER FIFTEEN ⪧

Snazz' Madoodle

Thomas Candlewick yawned and pushed aside the velvet curtain that covered his porthole window.

Beautiful onion-shaped spires and towering minarets sprawled below the Cornucopia as the flying submarine banked and flew toward the prearranged landing area.

Has it really been five years since I was last here? he thought as he gazed down at the glittering city of Snazz' Madoodle. He couldn't help but wonder if things would have been different with the Jinns if he had taken more regular trips to visit them. Maybe then the Jinns would trust him more.

Maybe it's not too late, he reasoned, trying to be optimistic about his mission.

"Hey, what's that?" Jonathan pointed to the top of an unusually shaped spire below them. It had a tiny, rotating golden weathervane formed from a concentric spiral. As it slowly turned, it reflected the glow of the setting sun.

"That thing?" Gene commented. "I have no idea. But I used to imagine it was a target when I was little. I'd fly up there and pretend I was in a Feathered Funicula chair and that it was an enemy from Curseworks. I'd spend all afternoon throwing rocks at it. When my dad found out, he was furious."

"Did you get in trouble a lot when you were little?" Jonathan asked.

"All the time," Gene said. "But mostly it was little stuff. Things between my dad and I didn't get really bad until more recently."

"Was it all because you started getting along with humans?" Jonathan asked.

"Yeah, that had a lot to do with it. My dad would fly home from Wishworks every day, flop down on the couch, and complain about this thing or that. Usually he blamed it on the Factory's *human* management." Gene glanced back at Candlewick. "No offense, sir."

Candlewick leaned forward. "Don't worry. I had many meetings with your dad when he ran the Jinn Union. He's a stern guy and a great negotiator."

"Stubborn is more like it," Gene said, snorting. "And he expected Jeannie and me to be like him and share his views of the world. He thought that humans were a dirty, uncultured race and had no sense of honor." The big Jinn sighed. "Problem was, after Ben and I flew together during the war with Curseworks, I just couldn't see it his way anymore. Ben became more than just another human to be angry at. He became my friend." Gene pressed a couple of buttons on the control panel, releasing the submarine's landing gear.

Jonathan remembered how Ben and Gene had fought together in a Battle Chair Squadron. They had made a great team. Gene's piloting skills and Ben's deadly accuracy with a Battlerang had earned them respect from many of the other more experienced fighters.

Gene continued, "My dad wouldn't talk to me after that. Kicked me out of the house." The big Jinn frowned at the memory. "Even Jeannie took his side. She's always sided with him, even when he's wrong."

"But hasn't that changed?" Candlewick shrugged. "I mean, it seems to me that your sister has been getting along with humans just fine lately."

Gene rolled his eyes. "You don't know my sister. She values my dad's opinion more than anything else. I think she just puts up with humans so she can keep her job at the Factory. My dad has a huge amount of influence on her."

Jonathan stared out the window for a minute, trying to think of something to say. After a long pause, he said, "Well, maybe it's just that your dad needs to get to know us humans more personally. You know, it could be that he's just a little old-fashioned." Jonathan rubbed an itch on his nose with his right hand, which was still dirty from the tune-up he had given the Cornucopia earlier. His greasy fingers left a big black mark across his cheek.

"Dirty and uncultured? Please! Give me a break," Jonathan said.

Gene glanced at the big mark on his friend's face and laughed. "Yeah, right. I'm sure *you'd* change his mind," he teased.

"You do have a point, though," Candlewick said, offering him a handkerchief. "I'm hoping that I can get through to your dad that our two races are not as different as he might think."

"Well, good luck," Gene said bitterly.

Two sets of runway lights appeared on the roof of a huge white palace. Gene eased the Cornucopia's controls downward. The submarine's massive wings stretched out for a gliding approach.

"Well, this is it," Candlewick commented as the sub eased into a perfect landing. Several Jinn guards approached the flying machine's door. Jonathan gulped when he noticed that they were armed with cruelly curved swords called scimitars.

"Are you sure they're expecting us? They sure don't look very friendly."

Gene snorted. "Don't worry about it. They always look that way."

≈ CHAPTER SIXTEEN ≈
The Key of Bone and the Door of Stone

"We here, Majesty," Snottrag, the leader of the troll miners, grunted in a gravelly voice. He bowed low in front of Penelope.

The trolls were unaccustomed to human speech, and the words were difficult for their coarse tongues to form. Behind him stretched a troop of forty trolls, all armed with pickaxes and wearing their lit kerosene mining helmets.

Penelope nodded curtly. "Good. Take me to the place where you found the key." The troll's red pinprick eyes darted to his assembled troops, and he let loose a stream of guttural commands at them in Trollish.

Penelope glanced over her shoulder at Preztoe. He wore a ragged cloak with a hood that partially covered the ugly side of his face, and his tail glowed a healthy green color, thanks to the food she had given him earlier.

"You can handle this, right?" She looked at the Half Jinn with a concerned expression. "It might be a long way down."

Preztoe nodded. "I'm feeling okay."

Penelope's heart beat with excitement as they followed the marching trolls down a long flight of roughly shaped stairs.

Once I have Abul Cadabra under my control, I'm going to blast Ben and that stupid Factory so hard, they're never gonna know what hit them. And then, after I've had my revenge . . . She secretly eyed the Half Jinn who floated next to her. *Maybe I'll make Preztoe my vice president. Wouldn't old Rottenbutt hate that!* She imagined the look on Rottenjaw's face and had to suppress a giggle.

The stairs ended at the Research department——a dank, underground cavern that was filled with more of her curse-making machinery and piles of coins that had been stolen from Wishing Wells all over the world. Several troll miners were handing bags of coins to Spider Monkey technicians, who then dumped them into a large metal sorter.

The Spider Monkey with the "too white teeth" was placing coins inside her Curse Meter one at a time and writing down the results on a clipboard. Penelope had ordered him to record what happened when a wish was changed into a curse. She also wanted to know how each coin affected the size of the curse, and how much time the meter would give each coin.

Penelope stopped the march to briefly inspect the results of the testing. To her surprise, the type of coin used didn't make a difference in the size of the curse. Instead, the results showed that the size and ferocity of the curse had more to do with the kind of wish made on the coin. When the wish was changed into a curse, its power was affected by how strong the belief of the wisher had been when they had made it.

This wasn't great news for Penelope. It meant that every coin could have a different result! How could she put together an army of really terrible curses if she couldn't measure how much wishing power was in each coin?

Deciding that it would be a problem for her to work on later, she ordered the Spider Monkey to keep up the testing and resumed the march.

They traveled beneath Curseworks to a secret passage that intersected Wishworks' Wishing Well Pipeline. The miners turned up the wicks on their kerosene helmets and marched into the engulfing darkness.

Penelope's hand felt the Key of Bone in her pink jeans pocket. If the rhyme that Al'Kazaam had written was true, then she and Preztoe had nothing to fear. She recited the lines of the poem that the Half Jinn had translated for her.

> *"Of mortal flesh, the Cursed Jinn,*
> *And Enemies' daughter shall venture in;*
> *There they'll see their heart's desire:*
> *My Master's Lamp dwells in the fire."*

"Enemies' daughter," she whispered to herself. *That probably means "enemy of the Jinns" or a human daughter.* She seemed to fit that description okay. As far as Preztoe went, she assumed that Half Jinns were rare among the Jinnish people. "Cursed Jinn" sounded like a good description for someone who had one human parent.

She glanced at Preztoe.

He looked back at her, and she looked quickly away. Up until this point, all the boys she'd ever met were idiots. But there was something about Preztoe that was different.

"*Thrakul growluk,*" one of the troll miners, a scout, interrupted her thoughts. Snottrag translated his report.

"He says all clear. No *grobbers*," he said, using the Trollish word for gnomes.

"How far down the Pipeline do we have to go before we get to the next tunnel?" Penelope asked.

"No too far. Close."

"Good. Let's go," she said, feeling anxious. The last thing she wanted was to run into a group of pesky gnomes that would report her activities to Wishworks.

The intersecting passageway that the trolls had dug split from the Wishing Well Pipeline at a spot fifty feet farther down the tunnel. Fortunately, this part of the Pipeline led to a long-abandoned Wishing Well and was seldom used.

If any gnomes came down this way, they probably went right by it, Penelope thought as she walked into the opening.

"Um, Your Majesty?" Preztoe floated up behind her.

"You don't have to call me that," Penelope said awkwardly. It was the first time that she hadn't insisted on being addressed with her formal title. "Penny is fine."

"Okay, Penny. I'm worried about the prophecy," Preztoe admitted, sounding nervous. "I mean, it sounds like the Chosen Two will be able to get past the Earth, Air, Fire, and Water hazards. If, by chance, it was referring to you and me, then I think we'll be fine. But what happens if it's talking about someone else?"

"I don't care. I'm not leaving without that lamp," Penelope said with more confidence than she actually felt.

Preztoe had to admit it, being with Penelope hadn't been as bad as he had imagined. The last president of Curseworks, Adolfus Thornblood, had been cruel and merciless.

This was the first time that he had been out of the dungeon cell in ages, and even if the mission they were on was dangerous, it was a lot better than being hooked up to the Curse machines.

Preztoe remembered the days after his exile from the Jinn Territories well. He had wandered through the Pfefferminz Ridge of mountains for days without food or water. He had felt like an animal, an outcast that was hated by all.

When the Curseworks Spider Monkeys had captured him, he'd actually been relieved. For the first few months, he was able to put up with the torture he experienced in the dungeon. What choice did he have? At least in prison he had food and water once in a while.

But in the last few weeks before he met Penelope, the situation had been growing intolerable.

He glanced at Penelope. She was probably about a year younger than him. And although he wouldn't have called her pretty, exactly (he was certainly not one to judge on appearances), she was the first girl he'd ever met who had not run away in disgust after seeing his face.

They'd traveled for about twenty minutes when the tunnel abruptly ended in front of a huge stone.

"Find key here," Snottrag said, indicating a shallow depression in the dirt at the foot of the big stone. "No dig farther. Big rock, stop."

Penelope and Preztoe walked down to the big rock and inspected its hard, flat surface. It was unmarked and had no evidence of a keyhole anywhere that Penelope could see.

"Read it again, would you?" Penelope handed the Al'Kazaam's book to Preztoe.

"Which part?"

"All of it," Penelope said. She hoped that there would be something in it that would give her a clue.

Preztoe opened the book and read.

> "*The words of Al'Kazaam, faithful servant of his Imperial Majesty Abul Cadabra, Greatest of Jinns, to the Chosen Two:*
>
> "*Seek fire and water, wind and stone,*
> *Secret locks and Key of Bone;*
> *There four deaths await the unworthy soul,*
> *Who seeks to travel the paths below.*

"*The first in the roots of cursed tree,*
The second awash in boiling seas;
The third, the howl of tortured stone,
The fourth will burn in fires cold.

"*Of mortal flesh, the Cursed Jinn,*
And Enemies' Daughter shall venture in;
There they'll see their heart's desire:
My Master's Lamp dwells in the fire."

Penelope had been staring at the stone the entire time Preztoe was reading the poem. There was something in the first part that stuck out to her. *Seek fire and water, wind and stone. Secret locks and Key of Bone. Fire and water. Wind and stone.*

She had an idea. Putting her mouth right up to the rock, she took a deep breath. Then she exhaled slowly, just as if she were breathing on a pair of glasses before polishing the lenses.

Suddenly, a network of glowing blue veins shot through the boulder. The lines were bright for a moment, and then faded to reveal a hidden keyhole in the stone's center.

Wind and Stone! Her breath had been the wind! Penelope

glanced at the stunned expression on Preztoe's face. Then, grinning triumphantly, she turned back to the boulder and inserted the Key of Bone into the lock.

There was a small *click* and the huge stone swung slowly inward, revealing a passageway. A loud hiss of escaping air echoed through the tunnel as dust and debris crumbled from the opening left by the huge boulder.

This is it! Penelope's wide eyes stared into the darkened passageway that stretched in front of her. A soft breeze wafted over her, carrying the scent of dirt and rotting leaves.

Suddenly, from the infinite darkness, four voices called out: "Who dares summon the Elementals?"

Penelope was too nervous to speak. She didn't like the sound of the voices.

Preztoe, sensing Penelope's hesitation, gathered his courage and shouted into the emptiness, "It is the Half Jinn and the Enemies' Daughter. We seek the lamp of Abul Cadabra, Greatest of Jinns."

There was a short pause, and then the voices rumbled in chorus, "Only the Chosen Two may pass. All others will be destroyed."

Penelope glanced at Preztoe, who gave her a questioning look. Up until now it had been safe to assume that Al' Kazaam's poem referred to them as the Chosen Two. If they stepped through the door and were wrong, Penelope had the feeling that whatever waited inside for them would have no mercy.

She stared into the darkness, wondering what she should do. Was going after Abul Cadabra worth risking her life?

Suddenly, a quiet, cold rage filled her soul, giving her the strength and courage she sought. All the years of rejection and frustration, all the years of jealousy and anger she had for Ben and his parents were now her source of power.

Preztoe would be with her. He had been rejected by his people, just like she had. The rhyme *had* to be talking about them. It was too perfect. She was the Enemies' Daughter, and he was the Half Jinn.

She looked around. The trolls had scattered at the sound of the dark, powerful voices, dropping their pickaxes where they had been standing in their hurried escape. Only Preztoe stood beside her now, waiting for her decision.

Gritting her teeth together, she said firmly, "We're going in. I need that lamp."

≋ Chapter Seventeen ≋
The Inventing Chamber

"*T*hese beds are amazing. What did the king call them?" Ben asked, stifling a yawn.

"*Togglenoggin's Patented Cloud Floaters*," Fizzle said with a grin. "Must be one of the king's inventions."

Ben reluctantly climbed down off the fluffy cloud-shaped bed that hovered over the ground.

"I got a note from one of the guards that said we're supposed to meet the king at the Inventing Chamber in the royal palace," Jeannie said, fishing out a letter written on stationery made from incredibly thin, beaten copper.

"Us too." Ben indicated the identical letters that he and the others held. "We'd better hurry." He glanced anxiously at his magic wristwatch and noticed that the birthday candle hands pointed at nine o'clock. Ben hoped that the meeting with the king wouldn't last too long. He was eager to get going with the mission.

The group chatted as they walked to the palace. But Nora was uncharacteristically quiet.

"Hey, you okay?" Ben asked, walking up next to her.

Nora responded with a small shrug.

"Listen," Ben continued, "before you know it, this will all be over. We'll be back up at Wishworks, safe and sound."

Nora didn't look convinced, but she offered Ben a small smile. Ben knew that the leprechaun was really anxious, and wished he could say something to make her feel better.

They entered the palace and walked down a golden-carpeted hallway lined with small copper suits of armor.

"What's up with her?" Jeannie asked Ben. She pointed to Nora, who was walking a few feet ahead.

"I dunno," Ben said, concerned. "She's acting really weird. I think the Elementals are really freaking her out."

Nora must have sensed that they were talking about her, because she glanced back at Jeannie and shot her an icy glare. Then she turned and marched forward briskly.

Jeannie shrugged and said, "Yeah. To be perfectly honest, it's got me a little worried, too." Jeannie floated up next to Ben so that their shoulders were touching.

"Well, uh, I'm sure there's really nothing to worry about," Ben said, blushing. "They're probably just stories."

"I'm sure you're right." Jeannie smiled and gazed at him with her pretty golden eyes. Ben tried to make eye contact with her, but couldn't. Knowing his face was probably a deep, beet red color, he cleared his throat and tried to think of something to say. He'd noticed that Nora was looking back at the two of them again, and that she didn't look happy. He wished he knew a way to ease the tension between the two girls.

"Hey, looks like our escort is here," Ben said, changing the subject.

A clockwork guard clanked forward and bowed, his curled brass beard almost touching the floor. They followed him to a huge metal door.

The guard entered a series of complicated numbers into a combination lock and the door swung open. Inside was an incredible laboratory filled with whirling gadgets.

"You are privileged, my friends," King Togglenoggin said, walking out of the fog with two of his royal guards next to him. "Not many top-dwellers have ever seen my top-secret, personal Inventing Chamber."[22]

"Actually, I can barely see anything," Ben said, waving his hand to try to clear the dense layer of steam.

King Togglenoggin chuckled and motioned for them to follow him. "We use a lot of boilers in this area. It will clear up ahead."

Ben and the others followed the squat gnome through the layers of mist to a vast chamber filled with ticking gadgets and long rows of workbenches. Gnomes wearing laboratory coats and goggles were hunched over their inventions, hammering, welding, and testing.

"I'm going to supply you with several of my latest clockwork soldiers for your trip. But before we get to their barracks, I just have to stop and show you this." The king indicated a thin gnome who was working on something that looked like a cross between a sprinkler and a fire hydrant. The gnome bowed and stepped back from his contraption as the king drew near.

"This is a little something we've been working on for about a year. It's a new way of taking a shower. When the

---

[22] In fact, the last top-dweller to see the Inventing Chamber was Bertram Snicklepants, the very large Wishworks President who commissioned the Gnomes to make a Feathered Funicula chair into a Feathered Funicula sofa so that he could ride more comfortably. His huge flying couch is kept in the Wishworks Archival Museum.

water comes out of the nozzle up there"—he pointed to the broad showerhead—"it is mixed with a special kind of bubble soap that has some amusing properties. It not only gets you clean, but it entertains you as well. Watch."

The king indicated that the gnome should turn on the water. The gnome positioned the head over a big sink and turned it on. Moments later, a torrent of hot water rushed into the basin accompanied by some of the funniest bubbles Ben had ever seen. They had grinning faces with buckteeth, and when they popped, they uttered silly jokes.

"That's great," Ben said, laughing at the ridiculous bubbles. "I think it will really make kids want to take baths. What's it called?"

"Bubble Buddies. We'll be debuting this device at the science fair next year."

The king, looking pleased, thanked the gnome for the demonstration.

The group continued to follow him past more workbenches and ticking contraptions.

"Hey, what's he working on?" Ben asked the king, pointing at one of the workers.

"The Battlerang Research and Development department requested a new modifier for the Battlerangs. When we've completed these new enhancements, look out!" The king grinned at Ben and winked. "The new Battlerang Blazer 1.0 is going to be incredible."

Ben glanced enviously at the sparkling weapon on the table. He wished he could have just five minutes to inspect the cool new Battlerang.

As they approached the end of the massive room, the king ushered them into a side chamber that was labeled "Barracks." Inside were about twenty or thirty clockwork soldiers standing at attention.

"We've outfitted these soldiers for your mission. They're equipped with digging attachments so they can help you through the tunnels."

Ben studied the robotic men. They wore tall pipe-like hats with the symbol of Tiktokket—a single gear—etched upon them. Their faces were grim, with long, drooping mustaches made out of tin, and their eyes shone. They were about as tall as Ben (which was very tall for a gnome), and they carried big packs full of assorted supplies and food stores.

"They're also equipped with a very uniquely designed weapon." The king indicated the big rifles with bell-shaped ends that the soldiers were holding. "Those are Blunderbusters. They shoot taffy bombs that, when stepped on, will make your feet stick to the floor. The sticky stuff will hold the target in place for about an hour." The king puffed out his chest. "The taffy bomb ammunition is my latest invention. Patent number 492."

Ben nodded his approval. He could tell the king was very proud of his latest accomplishment.

"Wow. That sounds really great. Congratulations!"

The king beamed back at the group. "I have some other things to give you, too." Togglenoggin walked over to a nearby shelf and removed a small, beautifully carved chest.

"These inventions are some of our rarest treasures. I hope you'll find them useful on your journey," the king said.

Ben felt excited as the king opened the small chest and removed a small pouch.

"First, something for Fulcrum Fizzypop's granddaughter." He handed the pouch to Fizzle, who accepted it gratefully. "Since you are also an inventor, I'm giving you these tools. There are lots of useful things, including a mining pick used by Surefire Poppycock[23], a famous Gnomish inventor. It is said that the pick is able to locate hidden treasure."

"Thanks!" said Fizzle, eagerly inspecting the contents of the bag.

---

[23] Surefire Poppycock (1771–1862) was famous for inventing many things, including Poppycock's No-Mess, Easy Grab, Rotary Nose Hair Trimmer, Surefire's Endless Toilet Paper Dispenser, The Cool Change-o-Matic Wish Coin Collector, and caramel corn.

"And for Benjamin Piff, a bottle of Whippy's Anti-Friction, Double-Distance Coating for your Battlerang," Togglenoggin said. He handed Ben a small bottle of brown liquid. "If you pour a little of that on your Battlerang, it will make it fly twice as far before returning. Some of our testers have hit targets up to a mile away." The king winked at Ben and said secretively, "The workers up at the Wishworks Battlerang Research and Development department haven't even seen that stuff yet. It's brand-new!"

"Wow, great! Thank you." Ben couldn't wait to try it out.

"Now for Jeannie." The king pulled a small, carved box out of his chest. "For you, I have a very useful invention called the Speak Easy. It will translate any language and record the conversation so that you can listen to it at a later date. It can be particularly useful when spying on trolls. Just turn it on, and you can decipher exactly what they are saying."

The king handed Jeannie the elegant box. Jeannie nodded her head and smiled, accepting the gift.

"And lastly, a gift for the leprechaun." Togglenoggin reached into the chest and handed Nora a small, familiar-looking object. Ben had to fight to suppress a giggle when he saw it. After all of the unique inventions he'd seen come out of Togglenoggin's treasure chest, he was surprised to see something so simple.

The leprechaun stared down at the object in her hand. It had two prongs, a switch, and a small bulb protruding out of the top of it.

"A night-light?" Nora said, unable to hide the disappointment in her voice. The little pink light had tiny frolicking lambs painted on its base. Ben couldn't help thinking that it looked like a gift for a baby's nursery.

"Er, thanks, I guess," Nora mumbled as she pocketed the tiny light.

The king gave Nora a kindly look and then said gently, "This light is more than it appears to be, Nora. Sometimes the darkest things are frightened away by the smallest flame. Use it at a time when you are really scared, and you might be surprised by the comfort it brings."

"Thanks for helping us, Your Majesty," Ben said quickly. "I'm sure everything you've given us will come in handy."

The king waved off his thanks. "Think nothing of it, my boy. I just hope you find out what's been happening with those Wishing coins. I really want them back as soon as possible."

Ben glanced at his watch. "Well, we'd better get going. The sooner we start, the sooner we can find the Thaumaphor and the missing coins."

The king activated the soldiers by flipping a hidden

switch on their backs, and the soldiers followed the group to the courtyard in front of King Togglenoggin's palace, clanking loudly. Ben and the others were given small packs that contained a couple of the metal picnic baskets that Ben had seen on the trees when they had first arrived.

They said good-bye to the king and set off for the nearest tunnel. Ben took the lead with Fizzle, who had her fairy light handy. Jeannie followed next, with a pale and upset-looking Nora next to her. Behind them, the long, snaking trail of clockwork soldiers clanked loudly as they walked.

"I sure hope trolls are hard of hearing," Ben muttered to himself. "Or they're gonna hear us coming a mile away."

≋ CHAPTER EIGHTEEN ≋
Trail of the Trolls

They had only been walking through the Wishing Well Pipeline for about five minutes when the clockwork soldiers struck up a marching song that echoed loudly all over the tunnel.

> *"Off to war! What a lark!*
> *Tramp, stomp, into the dark.*
> *Tunnels deep and caverns cold,*
> *We're shining bright like burnished gold!*
> *As clockwork men we feel no fear,*

> *We'll march forever and a year.*
> *Just keep us wound with springs curled tight,*
> *And we'll never fail you in a fight!*
> *Wa Hey!"*

"Please! Could you guys hold it down?" Ben shouted, trying to be heard over the loud song that the mechanical men insisted on repeating over and over.

Ben held up his hands for silence. His head was pounding. It took a few minutes for the command to reach the end of the long line. The last robot continued to sing loudly until he was sharply elbowed by the soldier in front of him.

Finally the singing stopped. "Thanks. I'm going deaf up here," Ben said.

"Tell me about it," Nora complained, holding her hands over her tiny pointed ears. "My head's rattling so badly, it feels like it's gonna fall off!"

"Wait up!" Ben heard a voice echo in the tunnel. Everyone turned, wondering who was calling after them. Then, seconds later, a small figure ran into view wearing a big backpack.

"Geary, is that you?" Fizzle asked.

The gnome nodded, looking embarrassed. Ben had to suppress a laugh. Geary was completely bald!

"Wow. You sure look different," Nora commented. Then, seeing Geary's eyes dart self-consciously to the floor, she added quickly, "But in a good way! You look great!"

The gnome looked uncomfortable, but he managed a smile. Then he cleared his throat and said awkwardly, "Is it okay if I come with you guys?" "I mean, if you don't want me to, I'd understand. I know I lied about being a great inventor and everything . . ."

"No, we'd love to have you along. We don't care about that stuff, anyway," Ben said kindly. "But how's your dad going to be with all this? Won't you get in trouble?"

Geary shrugged. "He doesn't really care what I do, at this point. But maybe if I can help you guys out, things will be better between us."

"Well, whatever happens, we're glad to have you," Ben said.

"What's that in your pack?" Ben asked Geary as they walked.

Geary glanced up at him and blushed. "I brought along some of my inventions. I thought . . . well, who knows? They might come in handy."

Ben remembered King Togglenoggin mentioning that his son had never invented anything useful. But because he feared that mentioning anything about that would hurt the gnome's feelings, he decided not to say anything. Who knew? Maybe Geary had a few surprises.

Ben took out Blastingcapp's journal and looked at the map. So far, they had been following the Pipeline. But now they had come to some sort of intersection. They could either continue straight ahead along the Pipeline, or they could take the tunnel to the right.

According to the map, they needed to follow the tunnel. Ben signaled for the group to follow him. He motioned for Fizzle to come up to the front and bring her fairy light.

Once inside, he was thankful for the illumination as they marched down the dark, low-ceilinged tunnel. He fingered the Battlerang in his pocket as they walked, his eyes searching through the dim light for any sign of nearby trolls.

At the end of the long tunnel, Ben noticed a flicker of red light.

He raised his hand, motioning for the soldiers to stop. With a sound like a dozen tin cans being thrown into a metal trashcan, the clockwork soldiers halted their clanking march. Ben winced at the sound, hoping that whoever was in the tunnel ahead hadn't heard.

He waved for his friends to gather around him.

"Okay, here's what we're gonna do." Ben placed the journal back in his pocket and glanced around at his friends' expectant faces. "The map to the Thaumaphor leads right through the end of this tunnel. Jeannie and I'll go up first and check things out. There might be trolls up there."

"But wait a minute, why should she go——" Nora started to object.

"Because I need you to be in charge back here," Ben interrupted. "If anything happens to us, somebody has to get word back to the gnomes."

Nora's sour expression told Ben that she didn't think much of the idea.

"Here, you guys, take some of this," Fizzle said, pulling out several pieces of gum. "It's Inviso-Mint. I'm still working out the bugs in the formula, but I think it will last for about an hour. Chew this and they'll never see you."

Jeannie and Ben took Fizzle's gum and began chewing it rapidly. Moments later, they faded from view. Then, to Ben's disappointment, after a few more seconds of chewing, he saw Jeannie come back into view.

"I guess it didn't work," he said as he stared around the circle at his friends.

"No, it's still working," Fizzle said confidently. "You can see each other, but nobody else can see you. Look at your arm. You can tell it's working by the faint silvery glow."

Ben looked down and, sure enough, his entire body was

glowing with a sparkling silver sheen.

"Okay, if you guys hear me yell 'Now!' that will be my signal that we're in trouble—that we've run into trolls. If you hear me, send the clockwork soldiers in to attack," Ben instructed.

A few moments later, Ben and the Jinn were creeping up to the source of the light. As they drew closer, Ben saw to his surprise that it was an open room lit with sputtering torches.

What in the world? Ben thought as his eyes scanned the room, taking in the numerous bags of coins and what looked like parking meters attached to elaborate machinery. Most of the bags were marked with an *X,* but there were a few that were still unmarked.

Ben stepped forward into the torchlight and picked up a clipboard from a nearby table. He read the scrawled statistics that were written on the greasy paper.

WISH TO CURSE AVERAGE: TEN COINS PER FULLY FORMED CURSE.
STRENGTH OF WISH MADE ON COIN DIRECTLY AFFECTS ENDURANCE TIME OF CURSE.

ATTESTED TO AND RECORDED BY: S. SPINCHLEY.

Ben stared at the paper, trying to figure out what was

written. Then, with a sudden flash of realization, it hit him. He picked up a coin from the table. As he turned it over and over, he read the writing on its tarnished, smooth surface: TWENTY SHILLINGS

Hoping that it still contained the wish, he pocketed it, and then turned to Jeannie and said, "Grab the bags that don't have an *X* on them."

"Why?" Jeannie stared back at him, confused.

"I think that the ones that are marked have already been used. Those wishes are no good anymore," he explained. "I think that Curseworks has stolen the wishes from the Wells and transformed them into curses!"

Suddenly from behind them came a low, guttural growl. Trolls! Shooting Jeannie a desperate glance, he put his finger to his lips, indicating that they should remain quiet. Maybe since they were invisible, the trolls wouldn't notice them.

But the trolls didn't seem like they wanted to move. Their burning red eyes bored into Ben and Jeannie, almost as if they could see them in spite of their invisibility.

Suddenly, a whirling pick flew through the air and embedded itself in the wall next to Ben's head. The big troll that had thrown it advanced slowly toward them. More of the trolls gathered behind him, hungry expressions on their horrible faces.

"Um, Ben? I think they can see us," Jeannie whispered, her eyes wide with panic.

Ben followed her gaze to his arm. Fizzle had promised them an hour of invisibility, but Ben was sure it had only been five minutes since they had started chewing! As he stared at his arm, he chomped harder on the now flavorless gum.

He could not see the silvery glow.

"RUN!" he shouted as Jeannie followed his lead.

They rushed back down the tunnel as fast as they could with the loud shouts of one hundred trolls clamoring behind them.

☙ CHAPTER NINETEEN ☙

The Negotiating Table

"**A**nd you expect me to believe this?" Gene's father's mustache bristled as he glared at Candlewick. He tossed Candlewick's contract on the elegantly carved table.

Jonathan gulped and exchanged a nervous glance with Gene. The boys were standing against a wall, far away from the table where the negotiations were taking place.

"I've seen that look on my dad's face plenty of times before," Gene whispered nervously. "All I can say is that Mr. Candlewick had better be careful."

Jonathan looked at the magical tapestries that decorated

the wall. They were covered with scenes of Jinn battles. The conquering Jinns stitched into the battle scenes actually moved, and were engaged in scenes of grisly victories over human foes.

One of the scenes showed a scary-looking Jinn holding up a lamp. Something dark and ghostly was emerging from the lamp's spout and was terrifying a group of human soldiers, who were huddled at the side of the tapestry.

Jonathan turned his eyes back toward the table. "You have my word and the word of the Factory . . ." Candlewick was saying.

Suddenly, Gene's father rose from the table, his smoky trail turning an angry shade of crimson. "YOUR WORD?" he thundered. "What use is the word of a *human*? Your people have lied before and they'll lie again!" The big blue man spat angrily and flexed his powerful arms. "I see no reason to believe anything you say. You're nothing but filthy slavers, and your promises are empty air."

If Candlewick felt threatened, he didn't show it. Jonathan couldn't help admire the way his boss remained calm.

"I truly understand how insulted you must be by Penelope Piff's lack of judgment," Candlewick said. "I'm only asking you to please consider the fact that she's just a child and had no real understanding of what she was doing. She doesn't represent the rest of the human race."

After a moment, the big Jinn spoke, this time in a quiet, dangerous tone. "I have heard your proposal, Thomas Candlewick. But the days of negotiating working conditions and salaries are long past. Imprisoning one of our people in a lamp is a terrible insult that cannot be ignored."

Gene's father straightened and gazed evenly into Candlewick's eyes. "My people are prepared for war. Your people have oppressed us for the last time."

Then he turned to look at Gene, who froze underneath his father's angry gaze. "And don't you ever show your face in these lands again. You are a traitor."

Gene watched his father stand up from the table and glide from the room. After a moment, Candlewick sighed and stood up slowly. The negotiations were over.

Gene and Jonathan followed Candlewick back out to the Cornucopia. The guards marched beside them as they left the council chamber, ensuring that they went directly to the waiting ship. The Jinns' expressions were cold. Their massive hands gripped the hilts of their swords so tightly that their knuckles had turned white. The message they sent with their body language was very clear:

The next time they met with representatives from Wishworks, it would be on the battlefield.

CHAPTER TWENTY
The Side Passage

"**N**ow, now, NOW!" Ben's voice echoed down the tunnel as he and Jeannie ran toward Nora, Fizzle, Geary, and the clockwork soldiers.

Nora's jaw dropped as she saw a swarm of angry trolls emerge behind Ben and Jeannie, wildly swinging their pickaxes.

"Geary! Make the soldiers attack!" Nora shouted.

Geary raced back to the assembled soldiers and switched them into attack mode.

The soldiers rushed forward to battle the trolls. The

shots of Togglenoggin's Blunderbusters cracked through the air, trapping the trolls in the sticky goo.

"There are too many of them!" Ben shouted as he rushed up to Nora, Fizzle, and Geary. "We've only got a dozen soldiers, and there have to be a hundred of them! We've gotta make a run for it!" Even though the taffy bombs were slowing down the troll army, many of them were still advancing.

Using the distraction provided by the soldiers, the group dashed back up the tunnel passage.

A pickaxe whistled above Ben's head and he ducked reflexively, holding on to his top hat with both hands. Noticing a side passage out of the corner of his eye, he swerved and led the group down the darkened tunnel. Distantly, he could make out the clockwork soldiers' battle song echoing through the caverns.

As they ran, Fizzle darted next to Ben, her fairy wings buzzing like a dragonfly's, and shouted, "I'm sorry! I thought the gum would work better!"

Ben shouted back, his voice coming in ragged gasps. "Forget it! Have you got your fairy light?"

There was a brief pause before Fizzle shouted back, her voice sounding panicked. "I dropped it back in the other tunnel!"

Ahead, Ben could make out the outline of another

passageway. He quickly made a sharp turn. If only he could see where he was going! He had no idea if they were even close to the route described in Blastingcapp's journal!

Ben glanced back as he ran, seeing swarms of troll eyes, like dancing embers, still following behind.

We're never gonna shake them off! he thought desperately as the small group continued running and stumbling through the darkness.

Suddenly, Geary's voice, filled with inspiration, shouted from behind them. "Cogs and crayfish! I've got it!"

Ben and the others saw the gnome wheel around and reach into his backpack. They skidded to a halt.

"What are you doing?" Nora shouted.

"My Handy Hand Warmer!" he answered, pulling out a strange-looking box and setting it on the ground.

Seconds later, the box started hissing and sputtering, followed by clouds of smoke that filled the tiny cavern.

Geary, grinning broadly, rushed past Ben and shouted, "It's a smoke screen! Come on!"

Ben was amazed by the gnome's ingenuity. They came upon another side passage in the tunnel and the group dashed down it. Ben was dimly aware of the confused trolls shouting behind them. Geary's smoke screen had worked! The trolls had been thrown off their trail.

But as Ben looked back again, he could make out a few blazing red eyes.

"What now?" Ben shouted to Geary. He could barely see the gnome's face in the gloomy darkness, but his jaw was clearly set with determination.

Geary stopped and removed another gadget from his bag. This one had a large funnel on the top, which the gnome quickly filled with rocks. He switched it on and shouted for Ben and the others to run for cover.

The machine whined like a turbine engine and suddenly started flinging stones in all directions. The trolls howled in pain as they were pelted with the rocks.

Ben looked around. He guessed they might have enough room now to use their weapons.

"Battlerangs!" Ben yelled.

Nora and Fizzle grabbed their weapons and threw along with Ben.

The three weapons glowed with white light as they hurtled through the air and found their targets.

"AIIIEEEEE," the trolls screamed as the Wishworks weapons hit.

As Geary's machine finished dispensing its ammunition, Ben turned to the gnome and asked, "What was that thing?"

Geary smiled up at him, his round face sweaty.

"My Stone Skipper! It never worked before. Threw rocks all over the place!"

Ben, breathing heavily, slapped the little gnome on the back. "I don't know why the king said your inventions didn't work. They're awesome!"

Geary shrugged. "I guess I just didn't see what they could really do until now!"

"What did you say that first thing was? That thing that made all the smoke?" asked Fizzle.

"My Handy Hand Warmer. It was supposed to keep my hands warm in cold weather. But it always got so hot that it would start smoking. My dad said it was stupid."

"Well maybe it doesn't work as a hand warmer, but it sure makes a great smoke screen," Ben said approvingly. "Now if only you had a flashlight in that bag of yours, we could see where we are."

"Hang on a second. I just thought of something we can use for light!" The gnome dug into his pack and pulled out a small box. He wound a key on the side of the box and moments later, the cavern was illuminated with a bright golden light.

"Ha! It's my reading light. Everybody said it was too bright to read by," Geary said, amazed once more that one of his devices had found a useful purpose.

"My grandpa always said that what makes a true inventor is the ability to look at ordinary things in a unique way," Fizzle said, flashing Geary a big smile. "I think he'd be really impressed."

Geary blushed and rubbed his toe in the dusty tunnel's floor. Fizzle swooped over and gave him a peck on the cheek.

"Gears and gravy," he muttered, turning even redder. "I wish I hadn't turned on that light."

Ben and the others laughed.

Ben studied the map in Blastingcapp's journal. While trying to escape from the trolls, they had left the main Pipeline and had taken all kinds of different side passages. The tunnel they were now in had just ended abruptly at a large, smooth boulder.

"It looks like a dead end," Nora said. "Maybe we should go back."

"Hang on. I want to check this out first," Ben said, staring at the rocky wall behind the boulder. He couldn't say why, but there was something about the wall that seemed strange.

He knelt close to it and inspected its smooth, flawless surface. It didn't look like an ordinary dead end. Glancing at the ground, he saw footprints in the dirt.

"Hey, guys, check this out," Ben called over his shoulder.

The others joined him and looked at the footprints by the edge of the boulder, one of which seemed to be wedged halfway beneath it.

"How did those get there?" Jeannie wondered.

Ben studied the map. "We took a lot of weird turns back there, but I think we've ended up in the right place." He showed the others Blastingcapp's map. "This line here," he said as he traced his finger to the place they were standing, "goes right up to the boulder and then stops. What if the boulder is some sort of door?" He looked up, suddenly excited. "What if it leads to the Thaumaphor?"

Ben jumped up and began pushing against the boulder with all of his strength. The others joined in, but the big rock didn't budge. After a few minutes of trying this and inspecting the stone's implacable surface, the group sank to the ground, exhausted.

There's got to be a way to move it. Maybe Blastingcapp's journal would give him a clue. He flipped through a few pages.

"Listen to this," Ben said. *"Stone doors hold no obstacle for me and my hat. The principles for making it work are so elementary, even a child could do it."*

Ben took the Clockwork Helmet out of his pack. After gazing at it for a second, he handed it to Geary. "If it is so simple, then why can't anybody figure it out?"

Geary took the helmet from Ben and studied it closely. He tried a few switches, but nothing happened. Then he looked at a worn metal plate that was on the top of the helmet. It had low ridges, forming a square. Geary's bushy white eyebrows knitted together as he gazed at it.

The gnome reached down, scooped up some of the dirt, and sprinkled it onto the metal plate. Then he took out his canteen and sprinkled a few drops of water on top of the dirt.

Ben and the others watched in silence, wondering what the little gnome was up to.

Next, Geary took out a box of matches from his backpack. He lit a match and placed it on the plate with the dirt. Then, to everyone's surprise, he held up the helmet with the flickering match, dirt, and water and blew a gentle breath of air across the top of the plate.

Click, click, click. Ca-chunk!

A low *whirr* filled the chamber as the gears positioned on the sides of the helmet started spinning.

Tiny doors suddenly slid open from a hidden spot beneath the helmet's brim. A pair of brass goggles slid down.

"Whoa!" Ben whispered, amazed that Geary had figured

out what all of Tiktokket's scientists had failed to. "How'd you do it?"

The gnome grinned up at Ben. "It was right there in the journal. Blastingcapp said it was *elementary*! So I figured it just needed a bit of Earth, Air, Fire, and Water to make it work. You know, the four elements."

Ben was impressed with how Geary had been able to see the simple solution.

Geary lifted the helmet and placed it on his head so he could look out of the goggles. He tilted his head and stared over at the boulder.

"Pies and pulleys," he gasped. "It *is* a door! And there's a message written on it!"

CHAPTER TWENTY-ONE

The Writing on the Wall

"**W**hat does it say?" Ben's heart pounded with excitement.

The group crowded around the tiny gnome. Geary's head moved from side to side as he studied the glowing green letters written on the boulder's surface.

"It's written in Gnomish, but I can translate it for you guys. It says:

> *"Through this door, prepare for war.*
> *Traveler beware, the Elements' lair.*

Pick the lock with Brimstone rock.
A breath of wind and then you're in.
All that glitters will soon turn bitter,
Follow the path, or taste his wrath."

"The Elements' lair?" Nora squeaked in alarm. "No, no, no!" She held her tiny head in her hands and hid her eyes.

Geary removed the helmet and handed it to Ben so he could see the writing for himself. But when he placed it on his head and looked through the goggles, he couldn't see anything that Geary had described.

"I can't see a thing," he said, disappointed. "Are you sure it's turned on?"

Geary took the helmet back and looked through the goggles. Instantly, the glowing words appeared. Geary shrugged. Bewildered, he passed the helmet to Jeannie, who tried it with the same result as Ben.

"It doesn't seem to work for anybody but you," Jeannie said as she handed the helmet back to Geary. "Maybe it only works for gnomes?"

"Maybe so," Geary said, putting the helmet back on.

"If Blastingcapp wrote that message on the rock, then we need to get some Brimstone. Does anybody know what that is?" Ben asked.

Geary scratched his head, thinking. "It's a kind of heated rock. My dad uses it for some of his most elaborate machines."

Then his face brightened. "Wait a sec. The clockwork soldiers have a piece of Brimstone in their primary motivators. I remember burning myself on it when they were installing them in the robot's heads in the Inventing Chamber. If we could disassemble one of the robots, maybe we could get some that way."

"What's a primary motivator?" asked Ben.

"It's a battery that's made of Brimstone and placed in the top of a clockwork soldier's head. A little switch on the back of its neck will open the access panel. But you have to be careful," Geary added, looking serious. "Brimstone is hot stuff." The gnome reached into his pack and removed a pair of thick leather gloves. "I'll be right back." Geary pulled on the gloves and dashed back up the tunnel.

He returned several minutes later, out of breath but grinning broadly. "You got it!" Ben said, looking at the steaming rock Geary was holding. "Were there any trolls?"

"None." Geary shook his head as he placed the glowing red rock on the dirt floor. "It took me a while to figure out which tunnels we took to get down here, but when I got to the spot where the soldiers fought the trolls, they were all gone. The soldier I got this from"—the gnome indicated the smoking piece of Brimstone with a nod—"was totally destroyed. Those trolls really did a number on the troops."

Geary removed a pair of tongs from his backpack and took the rock from the floor. "Now we need to figure out where the lock is so we can pick it."

"Didn't the message also say something about wind? '*A breath of wind and then you're in,*' " Fizzle said.

The fairy flew over to the rock and took a deep breath. Then she exhaled on the huge stone. To everyone's amazement, a network of glowing blue veins shot through the boulder, illuminating its flat surface. After a few seconds, the glowing lines faded.

"Look! A keyhole!" Ben cried, pointing to the center of the stone. "Now all we have to do is pick the lock."

Geary stepped forward with the smoldering rock and tried to fit it into the keyhole. After a couple of tries, he gave up and walked back over to where he had set his backpack.

"It's too big," he muttered as he set the tiny stone down to rummage through his pack. "But I think I can hammer it down to size. Somebody hold it in place for me."

Ben held the stone firmly in the tongs while Geary pounded on it with a hammer. Fizzle watched, impressed, as Geary quickly filed away the edges of the hot rock, narrowing it down to the size and shape of the keyhole.[24]

Geary moved over to the stone door and reinserted the newly shaped stone, twisting it carefully. There was a light sizzling noise and a sudden *click* as the lock turned.

For a minute, nothing happened, and then the vein-like lines on the stone's surface turned a deep, fiery orange.

Seconds later, with a loud scrape and rumble, the door slowly swung open.

"You did it!" Ben said excitedly as he peered into the dark entryway. A howl of wind echoed from somewhere deep inside, bringing the faint odor of sulfur to everyone's nostrils.

"I can't do it. *They're* in there, I just know it!" Nora gave a tiny squeal and dashed over to Ben, holding the edge of his pant leg with white-knuckled fingers. Ben had never seen the leprechaun so afraid of anything in his life.

"Hey, are you okay?" he asked gently.

Nora's eyes were squeezed tightly shut, and she shook her head. Ben disentangled her grip from his pant leg and, taking both of her tiny hands in his own, knelt down beside her.

---

[24] All gnomes have exceptional skill with hammers. It is traditional for Gnomish children to be given their first hammer and to be enrolled in blacksmithing school at the age of two.

"Nora, what's wrong? You've never been like this, not even when we fought the sea serpent. Why are you so scared?"

The leprechaun looked up at Ben with tears in her eyes. Her face was pale and her voice was shaking. "I can't do it. I've had way too many nightmares about the Elementals."

Ben wondered if he should just send the girl back to Wishworks. His magic watch was equipped with a button that could transport them back there in a flash.

He looked to Fizzle and Jeannie for help, but neither one of them gave any indication of knowing what should be done. Fizzle just stared at Nora with a compassionate expression, and Jeannie gave him a knowing glance that seemed to say, "See, I told you that Nora would be a problem."

Ben gave Nora's shoulder a gentle squeeze. "You don't have to go. I'll just zap us both to Wishworks with my watch and then come back after I drop you off, all right?"

Nora looked momentarily relieved, but then her expression turned anxious. "But what about you?" she asked quietly. "Who's gonna look after you in there?"

"I'll be fine," Ben said, patting her shoulder. "Don't worry. I've got these guys to look after me, right?" Ben looked at the other members of the group, who nodded back. "You've got my back, right, Jeannie?"

The Jinn nodded and smiled broadly back at Ben. "You bet."

When Nora witnessed this exchange between Ben and Jeannie, her expression hardened. The fear that had been on her face a moment before disappeared as she glared at the Jinn.

What's going on with those two? Ben wondered, looking at Nora and Jeannie. The two girls stared each other down for a tense moment. Finally, Nora turned to Ben and said, "I'm going with you."

"But I thought . . ." Ben said, confused.

"Forget what I said," Nora replied, folding her tiny arms across her chest. "I'm the assistant to the manager of Kid's Birthday Wishes Ages 6 to 12, and my place is at your side, Benjamin Piff!"

"Well okay, then," Ben said, confused at what had just happened.

"Let's go get the Thaumaphor!" Nora exclaimed.

ᔰ Chapter Twenty-Two ᔰ

Penelope Meets the Elementals

Penelope and Preztoe crept through a tunnel made from the biggest roots that Penelope had ever seen. *Who are the Elementals?* Penelope thought. The voices that she and Preztoe heard when they'd opened the door had been scary, and she hoped that she and the Half Jinn really were the Chosen Two. The Elementals had said that anyone else would be destroyed!

They rounded a corner in the tunnel and emerged into a giant underground cave. Penelope immediately coughed at the strong smell of sulfur. Squinting through the clouds of yellow smoke, she could barely make out the unusual landscape that stretched before her.

Gigantic tree roots grew as high as the ceiling. The cave floor was covered with dangerously pointed stalagmites— sharp stones that would do a lot of damage to anyone who tripped while trying to navigate along the narrow path that wound through the giant roots.

"Look!" Preztoe exclaimed, pointing to a spot just beyond the gigantic forest. Penelope followed his gaze, but she couldn't believe her eyes.

A gigantic underground volcano smoldered in the distance. Clouds of smoke emerged from its top, and ribbons of hot lava crept down its steep sides. Penelope had only seen volcanoes on TV. Seeing one for real was terrifying!

I don't like this place, she thought nervously. She was about to tell Preztoe that maybe they should go back when the ground trembled violently beneath them.

Earthquake!

Penelope and Preztoe were knocked off their feet. The huge root forest swayed back and forth, and many of the sharp stalagmites crumbled.

"Watch out!" Penelope shouted to Preztoe as a gigantic piece of rock crashed to the ground right next to the Half Jinn's head. Preztoe heard her warning just in time and rolled out of the way—he barely escaped being crushed.

"Thanks! That was too close . . ." But the Half Jinn didn't finish his sentence. With an ear splitting *CRACK*, the ground in front of their feet split open. The two scuttled back to safety, away from the dangerous split in the cave floor, their eyes round with terror.

Finally, the ground stopped shaking and everything was silent for a moment. Then four creatures rose out of the huge crack in the stony floor. Penelope knew they had to be the Elementals. They were the scariest things she had ever seen.

The first one was dark and small. It was hunched over and had long fingers that looked like gnarled tree roots. Penelope noticed that its skin seemed to be made of earth and rocks. And where its eyes should have been, there were only gaping holes. She shuddered with disgust as earthworms squirmed in and out of its mouth.

The second Elemental looked like a ghost. She had long wisps of nearly transparent hair and silver eyes with no pupils. A cold, cruel smile played on her blue lips as she stared down at them from where she hovered.

The third Elemental burned with bright blue fire that gave off no heat. He was bigger than the others and reminded Penelope of a Jinn. His head was a blackened skull, and an iron crown sat atop his bony brow.

The last Elemental stank like rotten fish. She looked ancient, and her gray hair hung limp and wet around her craggy face. The tattered remains of green clothing clung to her bony figure, and puddles of stagnant water pooled on the ground near her feet.

When Penelope's eyes met hers, the hag licked her lips and offered her a hungry, toothless smile.

"We are the Chosen Two, sent to retrieve the lamp of Abul Cadabra," Preztoe said. Penelope was impressed at how calm he sounded. She was certain that if she had tried to speak, she would have made nothing but a terrified squeak.

Preztoe stood and stared at the four monsters bravely.

"We shall judge if what you say is true," the Air Elemental said with a windy howl.

The four Elementals moved closer. Penelope shuddered as the creatures placed their hands on both her and the Half Jinn's heads.

CRACK! A bolt of lightning split the air. The little hairs on Penelope's arms stood up as powerful currents of magic coursed from the Elementals' hands. She was dimly aware of Preztoe next to her, gasping loudly as the same thing happened to him. The currents of magic felt like she had swallowed a swarm of bees that were painfully needling her skin from the inside out.

Just as Penelope felt like she couldn't stand it one minute longer, the painful sensation stopped.

There was a brief silence as Penelope and Preztoe stood in the center of the Elementals with their chests heaving. After a long moment, the Fire Elemental spoke in a raspy, grating voice:

"You are the Chosen Two. We will take you to where our Master waits."

Penelope was relieved. Whatever kind of test they had just been put through, they'd passed.

"Intruders have entered the cavern," the Earth Elemental suddenly said. He lowered his head to the ground and listened.

"A human, a Jinn, a fairy, a leprechaun, and a gnome," the muddy Elemental said, raising his head. The other Elementals grew agitated at the news.

"Brother and sisters, use your powers to destroy them," the Fire Elemental rasped. "Meanwhile, I shall take the Chosen Two to the Master."

"Ahhh." The old hag's voice had an eager sound that made Penelope's skin crawl. "I haven't tasted fresh leprechaun in over a thousand years!" she said, licking her toothless gums.

CHAPTER TWENTY-THREE

An Element of Fear

"*I*t's dark, but I can see some sort of pathway through these huge roots," Geary said, squinting through the lenses of the Clockwork Helmet's goggles. "I think we should follow it. Blastingcapp's message said, '*Follow the path, or taste his wrath.*' I don't know exactly what that means, but I think we'd better try to stick together."

"That sounds like a good idea," said Ben, who stood behind Geary. Nora was at Ben's side. Jeannie and Fizzle moved to positions just behind them. At Geary's signal, they followed him farther into the tunnel of twisting roots.

They followed the tunnel and then, to everyone's surprise, it opened up into a huge underground cavern.

Ben and the others stared in disbelief at the incredible forest of huge roots, stalagmites, and clouds of burning sulfur. Up until now, Ben hadn't been able to conceive of what obstacles might lie between them and the Thaumaphor, but as he stared out into the seemingly endless chamber, a shiver ran down his spine. The gigantic cave looked like something out of a horror movie.

"Wow! Check out that big volcano!" Geary said. The others looked where he was pointing and gasped at the gigantic mountain.

"And look at that big crack in the ground. I wonder if this place gets earthquakes?" Nora said. The leprechaun stood at the edge of the crack and looked down apprehensively.

"I didn't expect this," Jeannie said quietly.

"It's creepy, all right," Ben confessed. "But let's hope the Thaumaphor isn't too far down Blastingcapp's path." He turned to Geary and said, "You're the only one who can see the path through the goggles, so tell us where to go."

"Okay, stay close everybody." Geary adjusted the goggles on the magical helmet. He squinted through them at the magically illuminated path and motioned for them to follow.

The wind shifted, and the smell of sulfur grew stronger. As they walked through the forest of giant tree roots, Ben's eyes began to sting and water. Soon, he was having a difficult time keeping his eyes on the blurry shape of Geary.

"Hey, slow down a minute, Geary. My eyes are really burning," Ben said, wiping his eyes.

The gnome stopped and glanced back at the others.

"I can't see!" complained Fizzle, who had stopped flying and was now perched on Jeannie's shoulder, rubbing her burning eyes.

"It's probably the sulfur and ash from the volcano," Geary said. "I've got an idea. Hang on." The gnome reached into his backpack and produced a coil of rope for each of them to hang on to. "This way, we can all stay together. Maybe the wind will change farther up the path."

They all crept forward, hanging on to the rope that stretched from Geary at the front, back to Jeannie at the end of the line.

They proceeded this way for a few more agonizing minutes, and then Nora, who was walking next to Ben, took her hand off the rope for the briefest moment to rub her eyes. When she reached out for the rope again, it wasn't there!

"Hey . . . I lost the rope!" she cried, choking on the

fumes. But the others didn't hear her. Nora tried to open her eyes to see where they had gone, but the smoke burned so badly that she had to keep her eyes closed.

She took a step and suddenly plunged headlong into a maze of giant tree roots.

There was a loud crack, and seconds later, the earth split open beneath Nora's feet.

Luckily, Geary happened to be looking back and saw Nora fall to the ground.

"Nora! No!" he shouted after the leprechaun, but it was too late! The earth around their feet began to heave and twist, and a shuddering rumble filled the air.

CRACK! The ground in front of Nora ripped open wider. Moments later the long, root-like fingers of the Earth Elemental appeared from inside the big gaping hole.

Some of the clouds of sulfurous smoke cleared, and Nora opened her eyes. She took one look at the creature made of rocks and mud that was standing in front of her and screamed. The Earth Elemental was just as scary as she'd imagined he would be.

The Elemental spoke with a deep, earthy voice and pointed his long, root-like fingers at the ground next to Nora. "Come, my pets. Show her the terrible power of Earth."

CHAPTER TWENTY-FOUR

Earth

Nora screamed as the pincers of a gigantic slime-encrusted centipede shot out of the ground and closed around her stomach. Within moments, she was surrounded by a hundred writhing creatures, each emitting horrible clicking sounds from their insect jaws. This was her worst nightmare come true!

"Hang on, Nora!" Ben shouted. His heart pounded as he grabbed his Battlerang from his hip pocket. He couldn't see through the sulfur fog that surrounded the struggling leprechaun, but he could hear her screams and the sound of clicking jaws. Something had attacked, and he had no idea what it was!

Nora struggled to free herself from the powerful jaws of the centipede while the Earth Elemental approached. Her face paled as the terrible creature spoke, gazing at her through empty eye sockets.

"You have beautiful eyes, leprechaun," the creature said hungrily. "It has been long since I gazed at the world with living eyes. I will enjoy using yours very much."

"Nora, where are you?!" Ben shouted. He strained to hear where her screams were coming from. The sulfur smoke made it impossible to see anything!

"Here, Ben, use the goggles!" Geary shouted, giving him the helmet. Ben immediately grabbed the helmet and shoved the goggles over his swollen eyes.

Cooling jets of air rushed from tiny vents hidden in the goggles' sides. Although his human eyes couldn't see Blastingcapp's magic path like Geary's could, the helmet provided immediate relief to his stinging eyes. Far behind him, through the huge forest of roots, Ben could make out the monsters that were swarming around Nora. He grabbed his Battlerang and took careful aim, but he realized in an instant that she was too far away. There was no way he could hit a target at that distance.

Suddenly Ben remembered the gift that King Togglenoggin had given him. Grabbing the bottle of Whippy's Anti-Friction, Double-Distance Coating out of his pocket, he quickly uncorked it and dumped its entire contents on his Battlerang.

Then, without wasting another second, he took careful aim at the centipede that held Nora in its pincers.

WHIZZZZZZZ! The Battlerang shot from his hand like a rocket, glowing white-hot as it sped toward its distant target. Ben had never seen his Battlerang go so far. There was a burst of flame as the weapon hit the giant centipede. The creature screamed and dropped the leprechaun. What a shot!

Ben rushed through the forest of giant roots toward Nora, dodging the writhing bugs that lashed out at him with their razor-sharp pincers.

I hope she's okay! Ben thought desperately.

At last, he reached his friend. He picked her up as fast as he could, trying to avoid the huge, slimy centipedes. Out of the corner of his eye, he spotted the Earth Elemental. The creature rose out of the crack in the ground, hunched over and staring up at him with empty eye sockets.

Ben watched, horrified, as the creature pointed his long, creepy fingers at the ground. Suddenly, hundreds more of the gigantic centipedes exploded out from the earth around him, their pincers snapping hungrily.

Filled with panic, Ben scrambled back through the forest of roots and onto Blastingcapp's magical path. He could hear the sounds of the gigantic centipedes scuttling on his heels.

"Do something!" he shouted to no one in particular.

"Everybody take a piece of Zoo Chew!" Fizzle cried as Ben ran toward her holding Nora. Ben grabbed two pieces, and he and Nora started chewing as fast as they could.

Ben felt his arms shoot out.

"Nora!" he cried, fearing that he'd dropped his friend. But when Ben looked around for her, he noticed that his arms were covered with feathers.

He looked to the spot where Nora was and couldn't believe his eyes. He started to speak, but his mouth had turned into a beak. A loud screech came from his throat as Ben realized what had happened. Fizzle's gum had transformed them all into different birds!

As the giant centipedes rushed toward them, the group shot upward with a great gust of flapping wings. Geary, who hadn't gotten a piece of the gum in time, hopped onto the nearest bird's back (which happened to be Jeannie's), and was whisked upward just as the pincers of a centipede snapped at the empty space where he had been.

Frustrated, the Earth Elemental let out a roar.

SCREEECH! Ben felt a hawk's triumphant cry tear from his throat.

They had escaped! As soon as he had transformed, he'd felt immediate relief from the burning in his eyes. His new hawk eyes seemed immune to the irritating ash and sulfur.

Geary, who had the helmet and goggles back on, pointed downward, indicating that the group should follow the direction of the pathway below.

They had only flown a few hundred feet when Ben spotted a ghost-like shape hovering in the air about fifty yards in front of them. As they drew closer, he saw that it was a girl with ghostly strands of long, pale hair blowing around her face. His stomach lurched. She had to be the Air Elemental.

Ben desperately tried to motion for the others to change direction, but it was too late. The Air Elemental raised her long white arms above her head, and Ben felt the air around them change.

"SCREEEEEEEEE," Ben cried out with pain as a sharp blast of wind hit his wings like a hammer blow. The deadly howl of the gale echoed through the cavern. Ben's wings flapped uselessly as he and his friends spun down toward the earth.

Too strong! Can't find my balance! Panicked, Ben tried

everything he could do to fly against the powerful force, but no matter how hard he strained, he couldn't regain control.

Then, just as his feebly flapping form was about to crash to the ground, a powerful blast of wind shot out from somewhere to the right. The gust plunged into Ben's side, sending him tumbling sideways through the air just above the floor of the cavern.

The next thing he felt was a crashing *thud* as he hit a rocky wall at the back of a shallow cave. Strangely, he felt no pain. He knew that he had hit the wall very hard, and his head was ringing from the impact, but everything had taken on a hazy, indistinct quality.

I hope the others are all right, he thought.

The room was spinning. Then the lights around him dimmed and everything went black.

CHAPTER TWENTY-FIVE

Air

"Ohhhh," Ben moaned as he woke up. He tried to sit up, but his head was throbbing. Fizzle, Jeannie, Nora, and Geary were standing around him, looking concerned. And they were all back to their normal selves.

"Is everyone all right?" he mumbled.

"The real question is, are *you* all right?" Nora leaned over him, looking anxious.

Ben nodded slowly. "My head must have hit the wall when that wind came."

"We're all lucky that we weren't smashed to pieces,"

Fizzle said, gesturing to the cave's rocky entrance. "If you even try to step outside the cave, the Air Elemental starts up that tornado again."

"So I guess they're real, after all," Ben said, glancing at Nora.

The leprechaun nodded. "Yeah. And they're every bit as bad as I imagined," she said.

"Geary tried to go outside the cave twice while you were knocked out, but he was blown right back in again," Jeannie told Ben.

The gnome nodded. "It knocked me on my butt," he said, wincing. "I thought that the helmet would protect me, but it didn't." Ben noticed that his face was scratched and that the Clockwork Helmet looked a little dented.

"I wonder why?" Ben asked.

Geary shrugged. "I did find out something cool, though."

"What's that?" Ben asked.

Geary twiddled a knob on the side of the helmet. "I was curious to see if there was a setting on the helmet that would help us get through the wind. You know, like a force field or something."

Ben heard a loud humming noise emerge from the helmet, and he felt the little hairs on his arms tingle.

Suddenly, the Wishing Well coin that he'd rescued from the trolls flew out of his pocket and clanged into the helmet, sticking there.

Geary chuckled and turned the knob, powering it down. "Its magnet is almost as powerful as the one on the G. O. M. P.!" he said excitedly, handing the tarnished coin back to Ben. Ben put the coin in his pocket and grinned.

"Well, a magnet isn't what we need right now. We've got to get through that wind and find the path again. Or we'll end up like those other guys," Jeannie said grimly.

"What other guys?" Ben asked.

Jeannie motioned to the corner of the small cave.

Ben's skin crawled when he saw the two skulls grinning back at him, surrounded by a pile of rotted clothing.

"Okay, now that is *really* gross," he said, shuddering.

"Come on. There's got to be a way out," Ben said, wincing as he stood up. His whole body felt bruised, and his head was still throbbing, but he didn't want to waste any time.

The group proceeded to walk around the cave, searching for any loose stones or secret switches.

"So, how are you holding up?" Ben asked Nora, who was searching the wall below him.

The leprechaun paused before answering. "Okay, I guess." Her lips were pressed tightly together. "I'm gonna get through this." She continued to poke and prod the stones with her tiny hand as she spoke. "And after I do, the first thing I'm going to do when we get back up to Wishworks is have a hot bath and a cup of tea. That's all I want."

"I think I found something!" Fizzle's excited voice interrupted their conversation. Ben noticed that the fairy was using the magic treasure-finding pick from the toolkit that Togglenoggin had given her. She was hovering up near the ceiling of the cave, looking excited. "The pick started to glow when I tapped on a rock up here. I think there might be something hidden behind it!"

"Can you move it?" Geary asked excitedly.

Fizzle swung the pick with all of her fairy-size strength, but the rock wouldn't budge. "It's wedged pretty tight. I don't think I'm strong enough to pry it loose," she said, giving up.

The others felt helpless. How could they get up there? Jeannie was the only other one who could fly, but the space was too small for her to fit.

Ben didn't know why, but he was sure that they had stumbled upon some kind of secret way out. Why else would there be treasure hidden up in a corner of the cave?

An idea popped into his mind. Turning to look up at Fizzle, he said, "Hey, what about using more of your Zoo

Chew gum? Maybe you could turn into something strong enough to pry it out."

Fizzle brightened. "Great idea!"

She reached into her tiny satchel and removed a thin gray strip of gum. "Oh, no. It's my last piece." A look of concern crossed her face. "What if we need it to get through the other traps that might be waiting for us?"

After considering this for a moment, Ben shrugged and held out his hands in a helpless gesture. "I don't think we have any choice. We have to get out of this cave."

Fizzle nodded and popped the gum in her mouth. The others watched as the gum worked its magic. Seconds later, to everyone's surprise, the tiny fairy had sprouted pink, hairy, muscular arms and a high, sloping forehead. Ben grinned at what she had become: a pint-size pink gorilla with butterfly wings!

Fizzle grabbed the stone with two hands. With a mighty tug, the stone popped loose and rained a shower of dirt and small rocks down on their heads.

"Yes! You did it!" The group let out a cheer. Fizzle peered inside and indicated with excited gorilla gestures that there was something behind the stone. She pulled out a small, grimy pouch and flew back down to the others.

"Good job, Fizzle!" Ben said as he took the pouch and

carefully unwound the leather drawstring. Whatever was inside felt oddly shaped and slightly heavy. "I wonder what it is?" he said.

The others crowded around to watch.

"Here goes," Ben said, shaking the bag upside down.

"Eww!" Nora said, shielding her eyes.

Ben knelt down to examine the object.

It was a shrunken head!

CHAPTER TWENTY-SIX

Water

*B*en poked the shrunken head, feeling both disgusted and fascinated. It was just like the one he had seen at Snooplewhoop's Everlasting Circus.

"It looks so *creepy*," Fizzle said, wrinkling her nose as she stared at the black stringy hair braided with faded feathers and beads. Luckily, the gum hadn't lasted long, and she was now back to her fairy self.

"What's that sticking out underneath it?" asked Geary, bending over to examine the head more closely.

Ben prodded the head with the toe of his shoe. It rolled over, revealing a bit of dirty cloth sticking out from its neck.

"Hey, it's hollow," Ben said. He knelt down next to Geary and carefully removed the cloth. As he took out the fabric, he could feel something inside of it.

He unwrapped it to reveal a key, a brass coin, a tiny jar, and a bit of tattered parchment.

"Whoa. Cool!" said Geary. The others gathered around excitedly to stare at the unusual treasure.

"What does it say?" Jeannie asked, her voice filled with excitement.

"*Greetings from Phineas Crumpt,*" Ben read. "*You have discovered one of the shrunken heads of Limuw, placed here by the Thaumaturgic Cartographers for safe keeping. Use the key on the following coordinates: N34.07.174, W118.45.700. The coin and bottle of squid repellent are for your use, but please replace the head.*"

Ben read on excitedly, but realized that the rest of the letter seemed to be addressed to someone else. It said:

> "*My Dear Mrs. Crumpt! Why did Grandpapa have to die so soon? I suppose that's what comes from fraternizing with cannibals. Tell Rebecca, Oswald, and Little Sally that their father misses them dearly. I shall return when we have discovered the core of the Integratron and have seen that it*

is successfully returned to its rightful owners.
Keep the Key, Bury the Head, Drink the Light!"

"I wonder what the 'Integratron' is?" Nora asked.

"I've never heard of it before," Ben admitted. He picked up the brass coin. As he inspected it carefully, he saw that beneath the engraving of a large hand holding a shrunken head was a number signifying that the coin was worth one hundred Limuw dollars.

"The Thaumaturgic Cartographers," Ben whispered, and handed the coin to Nora. "I keep hearing about them, but I have no idea who they are. I wonder why Candlewick won't tell me more about them."

"Maybe they're crazy. Why in the world would they hide a bottle of squid repellent inside a shrunken head?" Nora said, gazing thoughtfully at the tiny bottle for a moment before placing it in her pocket.

"I haven't the slightest idea. But the real question now," Ben said as he held out the key and the cryptic note, "is how do we find these coordinates?"

"I've already got it," Geary announced. "The helmet is computing the location. It's right above those bones over there." He pointed at the opposite corner of the cave, behind the bones.

Ben and the others hurried over to where the gnome was pointing.

Ben knelt down to examine the stone.

"I found the keyhole!" he said excitedly as he inserted the Cartographer's key into the lock. The lock was rusty, but after several twists, it eventually gave way with a loud *click*.

Ben pushed on the stone next to the lock, but it hardly budged.

"Everybody help me push!" he said as he lowered his shoulder against the wall. With their help, the cave wall swung slowly inward to reveal a stone staircase that wound down to unknown depths.

"We did it!" Jeannie said excitedly as she stared into the passageway beyond.

"Wait a sec, shouldn't we put the head back?" Ben asked. "The note said we could keep everything but that."

"I'll do it." Fizzle said. She flew to the top of the wall with the small bag containing the note and the head and replaced them behind the secret stone. After she returned, Ben stepped forward into the opening.

"Stay close," he instructed, taking a few steps down the stairs. "We don't know what might be waiting for us below."

As they walked down the winding staircase, Ben noticed that the light gradually changed from the reddish hue in the cave above to a more greenish, watery kind of glow. He shivered as the air became damp and clammy.

"Wow, check it out! We're underwater!" Ben said. At the bottom of the stairs was a long, low tunnel with round windows placed in intervals along the stone corridor on one side. Murky green water surged behind the glass. It reflected light that danced on the opposite wall of the tunnel.

They all rushed to the windows and stared at the water. Ben was reminded of the aquarium that his parents had taken him to in Long Beach when he was little.

Suddenly, a huge shadow passed by the glass. Everyone jumped.

"What was that?" Nora shouted in alarm.

"I don't know, but it was *big*," Geary said with a shudder.

"Maybe it's the Water Elemental!" Nora said, wide-eyed with fear.

"Well, we'll have to face it, whatever it is," Ben said.

"Look!" Fizzle said. "There are more steps at the end of the hall."

"Then let's get going," said Geary. "If we have to face that thing in the water, I want to get it over with."

Geary led the group to the end of the secret passage and up a roughly carved stairway. When they emerged from the tunnel, Ben saw to his surprise that they stood near the base of the huge volcano they had spotted when they'd first entered the cavern. The water they had seen through the windows of the underground passage was a gigantic moat that encircled the bottom of the volcano. They would have to cross the moat to continue on up the volcano.

"It's huge!" Jeannie said, craning her neck skyward to see the volcano's glowing top. Hot lava flowed slowly toward the murky water at the volcano's base, hissing as it reached the surface of the moat.

Ben glanced backward and thought that he could just make out the spot where they'd entered the gigantic cave hours ago. It looked miles away! He comforted himself that even after facing the Earth and Air Elementals, they'd somehow found themselves still on track to find the Thaumaphor.

"Man, it's really hot!" Fizzle exclaimed. Ben realized he was also sweating now that they were closer to the volcano.

"Geary, can you see Blastingcapp's path on the other side of the water?" Ben asked.

"Yep, I can just make it out over there." The gnome pointed across the water to a rocky area at the base of the volcano.

"Well, anyone have any idea about how to get across?" Ben asked.

"Fizzle and Jeannie can fly. Maybe they could carry us across," Geary said.

"Maybe you and Nora," Jeannie replied, "but I think Ben would be too heavy."

They stood around the edge of the water, thinking hard.

Ben walked farther down the bank, his eyes probing the rocky shoreline. *If only there was something we could use to float across.* Suddenly, without warning, a huge spray of water exploded from the spot next to him.

The others watched, horrified, as a gigantic black tentacle made a wild grab at Ben. Before anyone could react, the tentacle snatched Ben from where he stood and dropped back into the moat, spraying a geyser of water at least fifty feet into the air.

"BEN!" Nora stumbled backward in alarm, her feet tripping over the rocky bank as she scuttled away from the terrifying creature.

Fizzle shot up into the air and searched for Ben in the water. Seconds later, she returned, panicked. "I can't see him anywhere! That *thing's* got him!"

"Hey, I've got something!" Geary, who was twisting the knobs on the side of the helmet, looked excited. "The helmet has a supply of air for diving in the water!" The gnome whipped the helmet off of his head. "But one of you is gonna have to use it. I don't know how to swim!"

"I can't wear it! I'm too small!" Fizzle said, looking anxious.

"Me neither," Jeannie said. "We Jinns can't swim. It puts our fire out!"[25]

All eyes turned to Nora. The little leprechaun looked terrified. She glanced at the water and then back up at Geary. Suddenly determined, she grabbed the helmet from the gnome and put it on.

"Turn on the air supply, Geary. I've got to save Ben!" she said shakily as she buckled the strap of the Clockwork Helmet beneath her chin.

The gnome pressed a switch on the side of the helmet. Seconds later, a protective mask encircled Nora's head. She dove into the water.

Down, down, down she swam into the murk. Soon, even with the helmet's mask, it was difficult to make out much of her darkened surroundings.

Where are you, Ben? Nora thought desperately as she swam. She pumped her arms and legs furiously, hoping that she could find Ben before it was too late.

---

[25] Jinns are especially uncomfortable around water and thrive in arid regions. A Jinn's heart can generate tremendous amounts of heat and is responsible for producing the smoky tail that Jinns float upon.

Suddenly, a huge shadow loomed up in front of her. Through the murky gloom, she could make out the hideous shape of a gigantic black octopus. The creature had the struggling form of Ben in its tentacled grip. Nora could see that Ben was getting tired. If she didn't do something right away, he was going to drown!

But what could she do? She couldn't use her Battlerang! She knew that this horrible creature was more than just an octopus. The awful stories she'd heard about the Water Elemental had said that the old hag could change shape. She could devour her victims in any form she chose.

Nora watched helplessly as Ben's struggles grew weaker and the last remaining bubbles of air escaped his lips. Her heart beat wildly as fear stole away her strength.

Do something! You have to save him! There's always hope!

The thought filled her with a tiny bit of courage. She fought to slow her breathing down. *Think.*

Then, suddenly, an idea occurred to her.

Reaching into her pocket, she removed the tiny night-light that King Togglenoggin had given her. Her face hardening with determination, she swam directly toward the huge monster that held Ben in its grip.

She was only ten feet away when she saw the hideous creature's eye swivel in her direction.

She pointed her arm at the creature's eye and flicked the switch on the tiny light.

CRACK!

It didn't have any time to react. The flash of lightning that emerged from the king's invention struck the creature full force. The tentacle that held Ben released its grip as the creature fell back, stunned.

Nora swam furiously over to Ben's limp body. She grabbed his jacket and pulled, swimming as hard as she could toward the surface of the moat.

He's too heavy! Nora was a very good swimmer, but she was much smaller than Ben. As she struggled to pull Ben up to the surface, she noticed out of the corner of her eye that the hideous octopus was changing shape. Seconds later, it had transformed from the water creature into the horrible hag from Nora's nightmares.

The ugly Water Elemental looked up and spotted Nora.

Suddenly, she shot forward like a torpedo.

Come on! Nora thought, kicking desperately upward. *SWIM!*

As she flailed wildly, her hand accidentally contacted the side of the Clockwork Helmet, hitting a switch.

ROARRR! A propeller emerged from the top of the helmet, shooting Nora forward like a Jet Ski, leaving the

Water Elemental far behind. Bubbles streamed around her as she rocketed out of the top of the moat with a tremendous splash!

They were at the other side of the bank in an instant. Seconds later, Jeannie and Fizzle, carrying Geary suspended between them, flew across the large moat to where she and Ben lay, dripping. When they landed, the three of them dashed over to Ben's side.

"He's unconscious," Nora gasped. "Do something, quick!"

"Out of the way," Jeannie said, moving forward. The Jinn put her lips on Ben's and forced air into his lungs.

A tense moment passed.

The Jinn pushed hard on Ben's back, trying to force the water from his lungs.

"Come on, Ben. Breathe!" Fizzle said, wringing her tiny hands.

Nora stared at him between the dripping strands of her hair. She couldn't lose Ben. He meant too much to her.

Please help him breathe! she prayed.

Suddenly, Ben started spitting out murky water.

Nora's eyes filled with tears. She rushed over to him.

"HE'S OKAY!" Fizzle shouted. The excited fairy started doing loops in midair.

After a huge coughing fit, Ben looked up into Nora's eyes and smiled. The leprechaun sat next to him, smiling through her tears.

"Thanks for rescuing me, Nora," Ben said weakly. "I don't know what I'd do without you."

= CHAPTER TWENTY-SEVEN =

Fire

Geary led the way up the winding path, carefully avoiding the channels of lava flowing beneath the dark cracks in the volcano's surface.

"Not far now! The readout inside my goggles says that there's an entrance up ahead with an X to mark the spot. That must be where the Thaumaphor is," Geary said excitedly as the trail wound higher. Since he was the only one who could see the glittering, invisible path, the rest trusted that what he said was accurate. They all hoped that the climb up the volcanic mountain would be over soon. The heat was stealing their strength, and everyone's throat felt dry and scratchy.

"Whoa!" Ben stumbled on a piece of loose rock and almost lost his footing. Hazarding a look down, he saw a winding trail of hot lava below the narrow path on which he was standing. "That was close!"

"Be careful!" Nora said, grabbing his arm to pull him away from the edge. The leprechaun gave him a stern look. "I didn't just rescue you so that you could go and kill yourself."

Ben grinned at her and wiped the sweat from his forehead.

"How much farther?" Fizzle croaked, her little voice choked dry from the heat.

"We're here!" Geary said, adjusting the goggles on the Clockwork Helmet. "I can see the door!"

The others joined the gnome. An elaborately carved, gnome-size door was in front of them. Ben glanced backward at where they had climbed from and realized that without the helmet to tell them where to look, they never would've had a chance at finding this place. It was much too small and well concealed. Ben guessed that he and Jeannie, being the largest of the group, would just be able to squeeze inside if they got down on their hands and knees.

Nora automatically tried the metal door handle and yelped, quickly shoving her smarting hand into her mouth.

"Locked," she said in a muffled voice as she sucked on her burned fingers.

Geary stared at the door through the goggles. "There's a message on it signed by Blastingcapp!" The gnome went on to recite what he saw engraved on the door.

> *"None may enter unless you be,*
> *On business from the Factory;*
> *Recite in order all the names,*
> *The dates they ruled, and their fame;*
> *Get them in order, make no mistake,*
> *Or a fiery tomb on this mountain make;*
> *This door will open for wishers true,*
> *Anyone else may not pass through."*

"Names and dates?" Jeannie said, looking confused. "Who are they talking about?"

Ben stepped up close to the door and touched it. It felt warm. He knew, with sudden certainty, that the Thaumaphor was behind this door. Turning back to the others, he said, "Isn't it obvious? It's talking about the Wishworks presidents."

He'd studied *Wishworks Presidents, Past and Present*, the historical records of the Factory, over and over again while he was training to become the manager of Kids' Birthday

Wishes: Ages 3 to 12. But he didn't feel 100 percent confident that he could recite all of the names and dates without making a mistake.

"But reciting all of their names and dates in order would be really hard," he complained as he tilted his big top hat backward and ran his hand through his mop of black hair. "I never thought I'd have to memorize all that stuff *perfectly*."

"You're the only one who has studied the book, though," said Nora. "If you can't do it, then we're done for." She looked apprehensively at the door. "I don't like that part about a *fiery tomb*."

Ben's mind raced as he tried to remember the order of the past presidents who had run the Factory. After a long moment, he looked up at the others with a nervous expression.

"I'm pretty sure I've got it."

"Just *pretty* sure?" Jeannie asked skeptically.

Nora moved closer to Ben and flashed him an encouraging smile. "Go ahead, Ben. You can do it."

Ben seemed bolstered by her confidence and, after a moment, said, "Okay, here goes."

He took a deep breath and, after closing his eyes, recited, "Cornelius Bubbdouble, creator of the birthday cake and candles, 1185–1200. Wadsworth Pfefferminz, who invented the Battlerang, 1200–1235. Wilbur Waffletoffee, who had the longest term as president, 1235–1310 . . .'"

Ben went on to recite each past president in turn, carefully remembering to mention the exact dates when they were in office. He was getting near the end of the list when, suddenly, right after Percival Pokenose, who had been convicted of spying for Curseworks, his mind went completely blank.

"Think, Ben. THINK!" Nora encouraged.

Snooplewhoop, Rumbleroot, Pokenose . . . Snooplewhoop, Rumbleroot, Pokenose . . . who comes after Pokenose? Sweat dripped from Ben's forehead.

"Look at the door!" Fizzle shouted. They all watched as the carved patterns on the small door began to suddenly change shape, magically forming a picture. Seconds later, in the center of the stone door, the face of an angry-looking Jinn appeared with its upward-curving eyes locked onto Ben in a fearsome gaze. Carved flames surrounded the picture and seemed to flicker ominously, anticipating Ben's failure.

Ben gulped.

"INCHI MAZ'BAHI TRUDO!" the head rasped, staring up at Ben.

"It's speaking Jinnish, but a very old form of it," Jeannie said, her face pale. "I think that what it's saying is that if you fail, it will destroy you."

"Tell it that I need a minute to think!" Ben said desperately.

"I don't know enough of the ancient language," Jeannie told Ben.

"Hey, I know! What about that translator the king gave you?" Fizzle piped up excitedly. Jeannie, having forgotten about the gift, reached into her pack and removed the small box. Spotting a switch on its ornately carved side, she held it up to her mouth and spoke into it, using modern Jinnish.

"M'nud M'hari," she began haltingly, using the modern Jinnish greeting. The box immediately responded by retranslating her words to the Fire Elemental on the door. The face nodded its head. Seeing that the door understood her, she continued talking in modern Jinnish.

When she finished, the door responded by nodding its head and saying in a flat, dangerous tone, *"Boochoo nadi."*

"It says you have thirty seconds," Jeannie said, turning to Ben. "If I were you, I'd think quick!"

Ben stared at the angry face on the door, feeling panicked. Thirty seconds! What if he couldn't remember?

He paced in front of the door, trying desperately to think. *Pfefferminz, Waffletoffee . . . Pfefferminz, Waffletoffee . . .*

Suddenly, with a flash, the next name popped into his mind. Relieved, he shouted, "Wolfgang Warblegrunt, destroyed all the Jinn's lamps, 1678–1724!"

Ben rattled off the rest of the names with ease, ending up with Thomas Candlewick. For a moment, the evil-looking face looked even angrier that Ben had passed the test, but then dissolved back into the pattern carved into the doorway. Moments later, the handle turned and the small door swung open.

"Oh my gosh, Ben, you almost gave me a heart attack," Nora said, giving Ben a friendly punch in the arm. "I'm gonna have to make sure you keep up on your studies when we get back."

Ben managed a weak smile. He made a mental note to brush up on his Wishworks Factory history as soon as he got back up to his office.

Ben didn't know what to expect as he crawled through the tiny door, but when he emerged into the cool, well-lit chamber, he couldn't believe what he saw.

"But it can't be," he whispered as he gazed at the endless rows of shelves. "No, no . . . this just isn't right!"

Neatly positioned in rows were endless columns of brightly polished lamps.

"So it's true," Jeannie said flatly, gazing around the room. "They weren't destroyed after all."

"Jeannie, you've gotta believe me. Everyone, Candlewick

included, thought that they were destroyed." Ben could tell that the Jinn was angry. Jeannie's smoky tail had turned the darkest shade of crimson that he'd ever seen. "We didn't know."

Fizzle spoke up. "But I don't understand. Why weren't they destroyed? I thought that Wolfgang Warblegrunt destroyed them all."

Ben shrugged helplessly. "Who knows? Maybe he couldn't find magic that was strong enough to destroy them, so he hid them in here."

"If word of this got out to the Jinn community, there'd be real trouble," Nora said.

They all watched Jeannie as she inspected each of the lamps in turn, looking for one with her family's Jinnish name written upon it in curling letters. Nobody in the room knew what the real name was except for her, and she didn't mention which lamp it was that she had noticed. Everybody up at Wishworks knew that to know a Jinn's true name was to have power over them.

Ben moved to the corner of the room, away from Jeannie. He guessed that her feelings about humans were probably not too good at the moment.

Spotting an old dusty crate that was tucked into the corner, he went over and sat down on it. How would he ever explain all of the missing Jinn's lamps to Candlewick? And who had brought them here in the first place?

Ben glanced down at the box he was sitting on and absently wiped some of the dust from its surface. He noticed that the wooden box was well-worn and that there seemed to be some writing on it.

Feeling curious, he stood up and dusted off the place he'd been sitting.

What was this? His eyes scanned the words that he'd revealed beneath the dust. *It can't be.*

Ben rapidly brushed off the thin layer of dust that surrounded the rest of the box and stood up.

"Guys!" he called. "You've gotta come see this!"

The others crowded around the box, looking at the spot where Ben was pointing.

There, written on the simple wooden lid, was the word Thaumaphor in big block letters.

"It's here!" said Geary excitedly. The gnome's happy tone broke the tension that had filled the room.

"Should we open it?" Nora asked, looking up at Ben, who paused before answering.

"Well, as much as I'd like to, I think we'd better not," Ben said. "Let's get it back up to Candlewick first. He'll probably have a better idea of what to do with it. And I don't want to take any chances now that we've got it."

Ben punched the coordinates to the Wishworks Factory into his magic watch. Grasping the wooden crate with one hand, he extended the other to the rest of the group.

"Okay, everybody," Ben said, giving them an exhausted smile. "Grab on to me, and we'll be out of here in no time. We have to be in direct contact when I press the button on my watch or you'll be left behind." Ben looked over at Geary. "You're coming with us," he told the gnome. "You don't think we'd just leave you here, do you?"

Geary smiled gratefully and joined the others, who had moved close to Ben and were holding on to his coat sleeve. Ben was just about to press the button on his watch when Fizzle said, "Wait a minute. Where's Jeannie?"

The others looked around the room. The Jinn was nowhere to be seen.

"Maybe she's upset about the lamps," Nora suggested.

"Jeannie? You coming?" Ben shouted. His voice faded into the deep chamber without receiving an answer.

"Let's go find her," Ben said with a sigh. "We can't leave without her."

"Jeannie, where are you?" they called as they moved farther down the rows of lamps.

There was no answer.

When they finally reached the back wall of the immense vault, Geary noticed an open door in the corner.

As he walked through the doorway, Ben was filled with an inexplicable sense of dread. There was something down this hallway that felt *wrong*.

He glanced at the others and saw, with some surprise, that they all looked as anxious as he felt.

"We shouldn't be here," Nora whispered as she moved closer to Ben's side.

Just a little farther, Ben thought. *If she's not here, we'll go back.*

As they rounded the corner, Ben saw the Jinn. She was standing as still as a statue and peering over a balcony carved out of stone. Ben approached her, still moving very quietly, and said, "Hey, Jeannie, what's the matter with . . ."

But the words died in his throat as he glanced over the railing of the balcony and realized what had her transfixed. A wave of fear swept over him when he saw the spectacle below.

It was *them*.

CHAPTER TWENTY-EIGHT
Penelope and the Lamp

"*Shhhh!*" Ben said as he covered Nora's mouth to keep her from shrieking. Directly below where they were standing were all four of the Elementals.

"I thought we'd beaten them," Geary whispered nervously.

"No, we just escaped them," Ben whispered. "I think they're a lot tougher than we realized." His eyes moved to the edge of the chamber. A familiar figure with long braids entered the room, accompanied by someone wearing a heavy, tattered cloak.

"I can't believe it," Ben said in an astonished whisper as he stared down at the familiar figure below. "It's Penny!"

"And she has found the Lamp of One Thousand Nightmares," Jeannie finished.

Ben turned and stared at where the Jinn pointed. Penelope was striding to the center of the circle of Elementals. A pillar, surrounded by flames, had a big black lamp sitting on top of it. Ben could tell, even though he was about thirty yards away, that the lamp was much more elaborately decorated than the ones he'd seen in the other room.

"Whoa!" Ben whispered. "What is she doing?"

He watched as his cousin and the figure in the cloak strode up to the pillar and stared into the flickering flames that surrounded the lamp.

"Who's that with her?" Geary whispered.

"I don't know," said Fizzle, noticing that the figure floated on a trail of gray smoke. "Is it a Jinn?"

"It's a Halfer," Jeannie said with disgust.

"What's that?" asked Nora.

"A Half Jinn," Jeannie replied. "They are not welcome among my people."

Suddenly, a strange, haunting moan filled the room. The Elementals were *singing*.

Ben's eyes moved to Abul Cadabra's lamp. As if

responding to the horrible melody, the lamp rose from the pedestal and hovered in the air. It soared just above the flickering flames and then floated over to the waiting hands of Penelope Piff.

"I've got to do something," Ben whispered desperately. He remembered the terrible things that Candlewick had told him about the lamp and the obsessed followers of Abul Cadabra that wanted to raise the evil Jinn from the dead. He couldn't allow his cousin to take the lamp back to Curseworks. She might try to resurrect the evil Jinn herself!

He wheeled around to face the others, who stared at him with pale faces. Ben whispered, "Look, I'm going down there. I have to stop her from getting the lamp. You guys wait for me back at the Thaumaphor. Once I get the lamp, I'll meet you and we'll zap ourselves out of here." He indicated his magic wristwatch.

"No way! You can't do that alone. You'll be *killed*!" Nora said, her voice rising in panic.

"She's right," Jeannie said, nodding. "We're going too."

"What?!" Nora almost shouted, threatening to give their position away to their enemy below.

"Shush!" Ben motioned for her to stay quiet. "Everybody just calm down."

"IT'S MINE!" Ben heard Penelope shout.

Without thinking, Ben rushed down a nearby flight of stairs and emerged into the chamber below. Preztoe and the Four Elementals all looked at Ben, shocked.

"Penny, I can't let you take that," Ben said.

"Now this really *is* a surprise," she said, grinning broadly. Then, turning to the Half Jinn, she said, "Oh, where are my manners? Preztoe, this is my cousin, Ben. He works over at Wishworks."

Ben flinched as Preztoe turned to face him, revealing his deformity.

"Look, Penny," Ben said. "You don't know what you're messing with. You can't take that thing back to Curseworks."

Penelope's smile faded. "You can't tell me what to do!" She raised the lamp above her head. "It's mine! Preztoe and I are the Chosen Two!"

Before Ben had a chance to reply, something white-hot sizzled through the air and crashed into the Lamp of One Thousand Nightmares, sending it flying out of his cousin's grip. He glanced up to the balcony and saw that it had been Nora's throw, an expert shot!

The Lamp of One Thousand Nightmares skittered across the floor. And then, suddenly, it flew up into the air toward the balcony. Geary was standing there grinning as he pointed the Clockwork Helmet's powerful magnet in the direction of the lamp. With a loud *CLANG*, the lamp flew directly into the helmet, sending Geary staggering back a few feet as it did so.

"NO!" Penelope shouted as Ben tore up the stairs after his fleeing friends. "GET THEM!"

There was the sound of thunder as the Elementals slowly turned in the direction of Ben and his friends.

"Go, go, GO!" Ben shouted to the others as they raced back up the hallway by the balcony.

BOOOOM! A huge crack split the stairs directly behind where Ben and the others had been running only seconds before. The Earth Elemental had its long-fingered hands raised above its head, commanding the earthquake.

Ben narrowly avoided falling into the huge crack. He glanced down and saw that the opening in the earth seemed to stretch to an endless depth below. If he had fallen down it, he would have been killed for sure!

Ben grabbed Nora and tucked her under his arm like a football as he ran after the fleeing group.

The earth rumbled and shook behind them as the Elementals gathered together the forces of Earth, Air, Fire, and Water. Ben's heart thudded in his chest as he ran.

Only a few more feet until we reach the Thaumaphor!

WHOOSH! A tremendous wind rushed up the chamber, throwing them all to the ground with its force.

Ben got up from where he'd fallen, stunned. He looked over his shoulder and saw the four Elementals slowly advancing toward him.

Ben glanced down the hallway in front of him and saw that when Geary had hit the floor, the Clockwork Helmet had flown from his head and ricocheted back toward the huge crack in the earth behind them.

The little gnome came to, and realizing that the helmet was dangerously close to the edge of the crack, stumbled to his feet to get it. He didn't notice that it was directly in the path of the approaching Elementals.

"GEARY, NO!" Ben shouted at the gnome, but it was too late. The Water Elemental had spotted him and was raising her bony hands above her head.

CRACK! A bolt of lightning cascaded down, followed by a downpour of slashing rain. The electrical force blasted into Geary just as he had fastened the helmet to his head. Ben watched helplessly as the limp body of the gnome was hurled through the air and down into the endless chasm below. It all seemed to be happening in slow motion.

"NO!" he cried, unable to believe what had just happened. Geary was gone!

Ben reached for his Battlerang. He knew all the stories said that the Elementals were practically invincible, but he didn't care. He wanted to hit them with something, to force them to pay for taking Geary.

He reared back to throw. Suddenly, there was a flash as another Battlerang flew through the air from behind him. Turning around, he saw that Nora had beaten him to it!

All fear was gone from the leprechaun's face and was replaced with a steely look of rage.

The spinning weapon sped toward the Water Elemental, who raised her bony hand at the last possible second before impact.

CRACK! A bolt of lightning cracked down and shattered the weapon in an explosion of white-hot sparks. The horrible old woman turned her watery eyes in Nora's direction and cackled loudly.

"NOO!" Nora shouted.

Ben grabbed the back of the leprechaun's shirt and dragged her from the chamber. "It won't work!" he shouted. "We've got to get out of here!"

Sick with guilt at not being able to help Geary in time, Ben and Nora rushed back up into the other room just as the Fire Elemental raised another attack, sending a stream of blazing fire toward them.

They barely avoided the burning blast as they turned the corner into the vault and ran to meet the others.

When they got there, Ben was shocked to see that only Fizzle was waiting beside the big wooden box that contained the Thaumaphor.

"Where's Jeannie?"

"She has the Lamp of One Thousand Nightmares," Fizzle shouted back, looking scared. "Geary gave it to her."

Ben looked around wildly. "But where is she?"

A rush of fire filled the chamber as the Elementals drew closer.

"I'm here, Ben!" Jeannie called down from where she hovered near the ceiling above them.

Ben looked up. Jeannie's hands were clasped around the lamp, and she was smiling.

"We have to go! Come on!" Ben shouted, waving for her to come down and join them at the Thaumaphor.

Jeannie looked at Ben with a pitying expression and shook her head slowly. "You really can't see it, can you?"

Ben was confused. What was Jeannie doing?

"What are you talking about?" Ben shouted angrily.

"Only that you've done exactly what I wanted. You've brought me the Lamp of One Thousand Nightmares! It was my plan all along!" Jeannie's face split into an evil grin.

"But I *trusted* you!" Ben said. He felt betrayed! How could Jeannie do this to him?

"And you thought I actually *liked* you!" The Jinn spat these last words as if the thought disgusted her. "You are stupid, Benjamin Piff! Just like all humans!"

"No, he's not!" Nora yelled up at Jeannie. "Don't you talk to him like that!" The leprechaun moved to Ben's side, her tiny fists trembling with rage.

Jeannie laughed. Fizzle and Nora moved closer to Ben.

"Jeannie, come down! You're acting crazy!" Fizzle said.

"Crazy? ME? You should talk. You and that stupid, crazy gum of yours," Jeannie said with a laugh.

Ben grabbed the Battlerang at his belt and pointed it meaningfully at the Jinn.

"Jeannie. I'm serious. Either you come down and stop acting crazy or I'll have to use this." Ben's eyes flashed with anger.

"My people demand justice! Did you see the lamps, Ben? All those prisons that were never destroyed? Once again, you humans have lied to us!"

Jeannie said. "And once I bring this lamp to my father, we will resurrect Abul Cadabra. Soon there will be no more humans." Her face twisted with rage. "AND NO MORE LIES!"

Before Ben could do anything to stop her, Jeannie sped out of the vault's entrance and into the cavern beyond. As the Jinn sped away, a crack of thunder split the air and the vault began to shake violently.

Ben wheeled around and looked back down the burning hallway. The four Elementals had turned the corner and had their hands raised for another attack!

Ben grabbed on to the box that contained the Thaumaphor and shouted, "Grab on to me, NOW!"

The others grabbed on to his coat as he plunged his finger down hard on the button on his watch.

CRACK! A brilliant flash of white light illuminated the burning vault as Ben and his friends disappeared.

They had escaped!

CHAPTER TWENTY-NINE

The Mysterious Thaumaphor

Candlewick didn't speak for a long time after Ben finished the story of their adventure. Finally, he broke the tense silence and said, "And did Jeannie say that she was going to take the Lamp of One Thousand Nightmares directly to her father?"

"I think so," said Ben. "It all happened so fast."

Candlewick sighed and gazed out of his office window. After a long moment, he said, "I'll notify King Togglenoggin about his son. I'm sure he'll be devastated by the news."

The Wishworks President turned to face Ben, Nora, and

Fizzle. "I'm very proud of all of you. You showed incredible courage down there. As you know, these are trying times for the Wishworks Factory, and you've all proven your loyalty and value a thousand times over."

Nora blushed and thanked him for the compliment. Ben knew that facing the Elementals had been one of the hardest things she'd ever had to do.

Ben wished that Geary could have been with them now. The little gnome had become a close friend, and he missed him already. Silently, he vowed to visit King Togglenoggin and tell him personally how brave and resourceful his son had been on the journey. He was certain that the king would regret ever making the decision to disown Geary.

"Now," Candlewick said, eyeing the wooden crate with a glint in his eye, "who wants to see what's inside the box?"

The others leaned forward in their chairs as Candlewick gathered a hammer and chisel and pried open the wooden crate. The top eventually came off, revealing a large amount of shredded packing material.

Like a kid eager to get to open a birthday present, Candlewick tossed the packing material to the floor and dug through it until he reached something shiny and metallic inside.

As he hoisted the three-and-a-half-foot-tall metal object

out of the box, the others stared at it in disbelief. Its shape was unmistakable.

"It looks like a big brass heart," Ben said with wonder in his voice. His eyes traveled appreciatively over the mechanical marvel, soaking in all of the details. "Hey, what's that for?" Noticing a clasp at the back of the heart, Ben gave it a twist. With a small *click* and a *whoosh*, a strangely shaped chamber revealed itself. "That looks just like the shape of the Impeacher," he said.

Candlewick nodded excitedly and walked over to his desk. He removed the little silver hammer from its velvet bag and brought it over to the Thaumaphor. Then he carefully fit the ornate silver hammer into the chamber. It settled into place with a small, satisfying *click*.

"Perfect fit," Fizzle commented.

Candlewick stared at the big brass heart. There was something about it, something that was tugging at his memory. Suddenly his eyes flashed with recognition. Without saying a word to Ben and the others, he dashed over to his desk and pressed the intercom button.

"Yes, Thom?" Delores's voice crackled through the speaker.

"Could you send up Jonathan Pickles? Tell him it's urgent."

A few minutes later, the door burst open. Jonathan Pickles and Gene emerged, huffing and puffing as they entered the room.

"I came as soon as I could," Jonathan said. "Ol' Purple Butt came along, too, I hope it's okay?"

Gene gave Jonathan a quick punch in the arm for the insulting crack.

"Of course," Candlewick said. Then, fixing Jonathan with an intense look, he said, "Remember when you were telling me earlier that there was a space in the Cornucopia's engine that you couldn't figure out?"

Jonathan nodded. "Yeah, it has a strange shape. Almost like a . . ." His eyes widened as they fell on the Thaumaphor. ". . . a heart," he finished, looking stunned.

Ben, Nora, Fizzle, and Candlewick nodded.

"It's the Thaumaphor, the third Wishworks weapon. We don't have any idea what it does or how it works. All we know is that it is one of the four weapons that need to be combined together in order to save the Factory."

Jonathan knelt by the big brass heart and studied it closely. He turned the device on its side and whistled softly in amazement. Spotting another small switch, he twisted it, and a second compartment, like the one Ben had discovered, revealed itself.

Ben and the others crowded around Jonathan to get a good look, and saw that the empty chamber that required a second piece. Ben stared at the unusual shape of this one, but he could make no sense of it. It looked like a spiral of concentric rings, each one winding smaller into the last.

"I'll bet that that chamber is designed to hold the fourth weapon. The Whirling Whizzy," Candlewick said as he gazed at the cryptic shape.

"Too bad there are no instructions," Jonathan said as he searched through the bottom of the empty crate. "I would love to know what happens when all the weapons are put together. Isn't there anything written about it?"

Candlewick shook his head slowly. "It is one of the best kept secrets of the Wishworks Factory. All the records say is that once they are combined, they will release the hidden power of the Factory and destroy its attackers."

Suddenly, Gene, who had been staring with extra intensity at the newly revealed chamber, gasped in surprise. "Wait a minute, I recognize that shape! I know where the fourth weapon is!" he shouted excitedly.

Candlewick turned to look at him with a stunned expression. "You *do?*"

Gene nodded his head and grinned. "We flew over it in the Cornucopia when we went on the diplomatic mission.

It's the spiral I used for target practice on the capitol building when I was a little kid, I'm sure of it!"

"That spiral was a gift given to the Jinns after the First Wishworks War. It was given by President Thicklepick to represent a symbol of goodwill between humans and Jinns." Candlewick's jubilant expression grew serious. "Are you absolutely sure it's the same shape as the one in the Thaumaphor?"

Gene nodded. "Absolutely," he said. "I've seen it up close a million times."

Candlewick stood up and paced around the office, looking anxious.

"Well, the good news is that we know where it is." He sat down on the edge of his desk and looked at each of them in turn. "But the bad news is that there has never been a more dangerous place for a Wishworks employee to travel to than the Jinn Territories at this time."

He sighed and ran his fingers through his prematurely white hair. When he looked at them again, his jaw was set and his eyes flashed with determination.

"With the possibility of Abul Cadabra being raised from the dead, now, more than ever, we need those four weapons. Getting the Whirling Whizzy is going to be our most perilous mission yet."

Gene and Jonathan, who were hearing the news about the Lamp of One Thousand Nightmares for the first time, looked shocked.

"What? Abul Cadabra?" Gene looked frightened.

"I'll tell you all about it," Fizzle said, putting a tiny hand on Gene's shoulder. "And there's something you need to know about your sister."

Gene and Jonathan stayed in Candlewick's office to hear Fizzle tell the story as the others filed out of the room.

As Ben and Nora left Candlewick's office, Ben was troubled about the upcoming weeks. Would they be able to stop the Jinns from resurrecting Abul Cadabra? Not only that, he dreaded the letter that he'd have to write to King Togglenoggin explaining what had happened to Geary and the stolen Wishing Well coins.

Nora interrupted his melancholy mood. "Hey, how 'bout some Battlerang drills?" The leprechaun smiled mischievously. "I think you still owe me from the bet we made last time we had target practice. What do you say to best two out of three?"

"I dunno," Ben said, with a tinge of sadness. "I guess I'm not much in the mood. I'll pay up now." He reached into his pocket to search for some change. As he pulled his hand out, he noticed that he was holding an unusual coin. With a flash of realization, he saw that it was the Wishing Well coin that he'd rescued from the bags of coins that Penelope was processing into curses.

A big smile spread over his face. He turned to Nora and said, "On second thought, I'll have to owe ya. Let's go and make somebody's wish come true."

CHAPTER THIRTY

Wishing Well

Mahdi watched as his father poured the last remaining drops of water from the plastic jug into the battered tin cup. His sister Nathifa's whimpers had been growing weaker and weaker every day. Even though his own throat ached and burned, he was glad that his Abu was giving the water to his baby sister. It meant that she would be with him a little while longer.

He had stopped running two days ago, and had stopped walking yesterday. Today he hadn't even the strength to move from his mat in their tiny house. It seemed to Mahdi that the scorching sun sucked at his very bones.

But my wish is coming. Mahdi's mind embraced the happy thought. *And then there will be water for everybody, even the cows.* The thought of so much water made him smile, his white teeth showing like bleached stones in his dusty, parchment-like face.

Suddenly someone outside shouted. It took all of Mahdi's strength to raise himself up on his elbow and listen to the excited voices that were coming closer to his hut.

A fist pounded on the door. Mahdi watched his father move to answer it.

"Yes?"

"It's a miracle!" Mahdi saw a pair of hands shove a huge plastic jug that sloshed with water into his father's hands.

"What's this?" asked his father, staring at the huge container with uncomprehending eyes.

"Water! Today, water has come back to Kumahumato! The well is overflowing! Get your bucket. There is a celebration down by the well, and everyone is getting wet!"

Mahdi's father smiled at the man, and his eyes filled with the last moisture left in his dry body. He took the jug, poured a huge cupful, and brought it over to Mahdi.

The water was cool and delicious on Mahdi's tongue. When the cup was empty, his father filled it again and Mahdi drank even more deeply, quenching the brush fire that had burned in his throat for so long.

After his father had taken a long drink for himself, Mahdi flashed him a big smile. His drained his cup and smiled back.

"Ahh. That is good," he said, staring into the bottom of the empty cup. Mahdi sat up and leaned into his father, wrapping his thin arms as far as he could around his middle. His father's big hand rested on his back and moved gently up and down in response. After a moment, Mahdi spoke.

"Now do you see, Abu?"

His father turned and looked at him with a gently questioning expression.

Mahdi stared up into his father's kind brown eyes. Eyes that no longer looked so tired. "Wishes *do* come true."

≋*Appendix*≋

The Gnomish Table of the Elements

Elements discovered while digging in the Wishing Well Pipeline

Fr	Su	Jb	Sn
1	2	3	4
Pu	Mo	Br	Sk
5	6	7	8
St	Bg	Ti	Bm
9	10	11	12
Ch	Co	Ft	Su
13	14	15	16

1. Element of Fear: This Element is usually found in dark caves with spiderwebs.

2. Element of Surprise: This Element is found wherever it is least expected.

3. Jabberonium: Element possessing strangely addictive properties in humans. Used in cell phones. Humans affected by Jabberonium talk constantly.

4. Snickerinium: Element that produces hysterical giggling when combined with Stupidium.

5. Putronium: The smelliest Element. Is easily located by its characteristic scent of rotten cabbage.
6. Motivatium: When combined with water, produces an energy enhancing formula.
7. Brimstone: Rare Element, used as a power source for complicated machinery, such as robots.
8. Sneakinium: Elusive Element that is often used for people who like to hide and discover secrets.
9. Stupidium: Exposure to this Element can cause very silly behavior.
10. Boogeronium: Element that has no practical value whatsoever.
11. Tinyinium: Smallest of the Elements. Most Gnomish miners have to use magnifying glasses to locate it.
12. Boominium: Highly explosive Element. Used in cannons and artillery.
13. Chickenium: This Element causes Gnomish miners to run away and hide. The reasons for this are undiscovered. No miners have been able to get close enough to it to do research.
14. Chocotonium: Delicious Element that can be eaten directly out of the ground. Especially good on ice-cream sundaes.
15. Featherinium: Element used in flying machines. Very

light, and can usually be found floating near cave ceilings.

16. Sunshinium: Very bright Element. Used in flashlights and lamps. Many Gnomes carry a small piece of sunshinium in their pockets on rainy days.